Acknowledgements

Thank you God, for blessing me with this gift to write and bless others.

Thanks to my beautiful Mother Bridget Lee, for always praying for
me and believing in my gift as a novelist. I love and thank God for
you.

Thank you to my Sister- Tonesia Lee, for being the best sister a
guy could ever have. I love you sis.

Thanks to my God Sister and Best friend of 19 years, Krystal D.
Davis. I appreciate all of your advice, prayers, encouragement,
and most of all the LAUGHS! God put us together for a reason. I
love you.

Thank you, Jemario Cooper (JLmarc). I appreciate those late-night
"pep talks" when I wanted to throw my lap top into the trash. Your
words of encouragement are greatly appreciated. Thanks for
always keeping it real.

Thank you Akeem Vance for believing in "Annabelle" when it was
just a movie script. Thank you for encouraging me to write the
novel. You were right.

Thanks to Lexi Bradshaw for your wonderful advice on "Brand
 Building". You are going places girl.

Thanks to the Spiritual Leaders in my life- Bishop O.C. Allen III,
Bishop Paul Morton, and Dr. Rick V. Layton. Thank you very
much for your inspirational sermons and teachings

A Special Thanks to my Grandmother, Ora Gillis. Thank you for
your prayers. I LOVE YOU.

Thanks to my God Father, Torris Williams. I appreciate all those times you pulled me out of a "jam". Thanks for being a wonderful
father figure.

Thank you Jeremiah Bean; for bringing your gift of music into my
life. I appreciate your advice, coaching and friendship. I will see
you at the top brother!

Thank you, Rozilyn Hunter. Those "carry-out" meals helped out a
lot. I appreciate you very, very much!

Thanks to my Aunts- Laura, Katie, Mary-Jewel and
Faye-Anne. You all have played special roles in my life.
I love and appreciate
you.

Thanks to my Uncles- Bruce, Leonard, Stephen, and Michael. I
appreciate you for being strong role models in my life..

Thanks to my Distinguished Brothers- Matthew Summerall, Chase
Mitchell, and Jermaine Johnson. You were all there for me when it
 really counted; love you fellas!

Thank you to my Creative Writing Professor- Joyce Cottingham. I
appreciate your wisdom inside and outside of the classroom.

Thanks to my God Brother, Carlos Taylor. Those motivated conversations at work really paid off and kept me uplifted. I love you man!

Thank you to my homeboys- Glen Carlile, Neville Grimmett,
Antoine Addison, Maurice Patterson, Robert Gilmer, James "JJ" Gaither, William Wright, Terrance Bryant, Henry Lee Jr., Rocky
Jefferson, Shawn Williams, Nick Smith, D.Bernard Wilson, Curtis
Callwood, Albert McClutcheon III, Morris Stewart, Keith Clark and Markus Chatman. Thanks for always having my back.

Thanks to a very special lady, Alexis Clemons. I appreciate those deep conversations and bright ideas that we shared while at work.

Thanks to my Personal Trainer and Close Friend of 12 years, Delroy Lee. I appreciate your motivation, encouragement and friendship; love you man.

Thank you Tyree Conyers and Jyoba Matacaumbo for always keeping it real with me, I love you guys.

Special thanks to Anita Gnon for being the model on my book cover. Thank you for believing in my vision. I love you girl.

A Special, Special thanks to Ms. Siquoyia Blue of "Siquoyia Blue Entertainment", Atlanta Georgia. This book would not be possible if it weren't for you coming into my life and inspiring me. I thank God for allowing our paths to cross. Keep doing your thing girl. You are full of gifts and talents. I love you!

I

Maryrose was nervous and frightened. It was May 18, 1833 at the Williamsburg Plantation. She stood closely beside her husband Daniel, and her older brother McAuthor at a memorial service. It was extremely humid that day in Tuscaloosa Alabama which caused the situation in that moment to be more unbearable. Tears formed in Maryrose's eyes and pain rested in her heart as she stood there trembling nervously; positioning herself in one spot and digging her three inch slippers into the dirt.

She gently rubbed her stomach which carried her first born baby, and gazed upon the beautiful flowers that she personally hand-picked. For a moment, she envisioned her mother being in a much better place feeling love and contentment. In times like these, positive thoughts were the only remedy to cure Maryrose of her sadness.

Cora-Lynn Williamsburg, who lied there peacefully in her favorite pink dress, was the guest of honor for the occasion, and the reason for everyone's attendance. Even though her children, Maryrose and McAuthor were left with a large inheritance; they were heartbroken because they suffered the loss of both their mother and father.

Confusion only haunted one individual, Maryrose. As she looked around at all of her family, friends, and loved ones; she could not help but wonder to herself, how would she take care of her child without her mothers' guidance? Who would help her with complicated questions she often asked herself? Would Daniel be able to help her as he promised? Would he spend more time traveling out of town, or in the Slave Quarters? These questions Maryrose asked herself frequently as she witnessed her mother fight for her life day after day until she died. Now that the moment had arrived for her to say farewell; she observed herself feeling more saddened than ever.

As service ended with a prayer in unison, people began to slowly depart from the site. Daniel turned to Maryrose and looked at her face; he wiped the tears from her eyes. A feeling of comfort overcame her spirit, causing her to feel more protected from the fears that imprisoned her for so long. As more tears fell from her eyes, she felt a certain urge to express to him the issues that had been troubling her for months. She gently grabbed him by the hand, cleared her throat to appease the trembling that overwhelmed her from crying; she looked up to him and said,

"Keep asking myself how I'm gone raise our baby. Mama's gone and I don't know a thang bout raising a chile, notta thang! What are we goin to do? How can we watch over the Plantation, the Slaves, the crops, and, and, and, whose gonna........"

Daniel immediately interrupted her before she began to panic; his intentions were to make her feel calm at the situations that they were facing,

"Not to worry sweetheart" he replied, "Have already arranged to have a Winch from the Quarters to help out, she's also wit chile and very capable of handling the task."

A feeling of anxiety overcame Maryrose; her heart began beating steadily at the sound of Daniel's idea. Could he be speaking of the same person whom he spent his time with night after night in the Quarters? Is her husband really considering moving his bed Slave into their home to help raise their first child? Maryrose wanted to cry harder; but instead she held back her tears, and replaced them with rage. She was angry at Daniel, and angry at the female Slave who unintentionally took her husbands' attention away. Maryrose attitude changed; she immediately snatched her hand away from Daniel and spoke in a harsh tone,

"A WINCH SLAVE, can't have some nigger from the Quarters come into our home to help watch over our baby!"

Daniel instantly observed Maryrose's change of posture, he was well aware that she was unhappy with him spending time away from home and in the Quarters. He was also aware that Maryrose loved him deeply, and would remain humble to his authority as her husband. Daniel smiled, leaned over toward her, and gave soft kisses on her cheek in hopes of winning her over with his decision,

"She will help out wit cookin, cleanin, and raising our baby." he replied, "Everything will be jus fine, as it always has been, we were raised by niggers in the home, we turned out jus fine didn't we? And so shall our children, now come along darling; let's not keep our guest waiting."

Daniel walked away from Maryrose with a feeling of triumph. She stood there alone with tears building in her eyes and anxiety in her heart for the unknown. Maryrose knew that deep inside, Daniel loved her, but why did he have this strange urge to sleep with female Slaves in the Quarters? In her mind, it was disgusting, and un-becoming of a southern white gentleman to indulge in that kind of activity. The thought of her husband sleeping with a Slave made her sick to the stomach. Although Maryrose was disturbed in her heart, she understood her position. Daniel was her husband and she was raised to believe that a woman's place is by her husbands' side, through good and bad times; to never question his authority, but honor and obey him.

Maryrose began walking slowly toward the wagon where Daniel sat patiently waiting for her. The further she walked away from the burial site, the more frightened she became. She knew that once she climbed into that wagon, and drove away with her husband, that she was not only saying good-bye to her old life with her mother; but saying hello to a new life awaiting her back home at Williamsburg, a life that she must be prepared for.

As Daniel and Maryrose were heading home, barely speaking to one another; Maryrose's mind was congested with questions and concerns about their current circumstances. Even though she wanted to continue the conversation that they shared at the burial site, she chose to remain silent and unvoiced. They were only moments away from greeting their family and friends back home, she did not want her attitude to cause any of them to feel un-welcomed.

Meanwhile, back at Williamsburg, the Slaves were down in the sugarcane fields working and gossiping. They spoke about Cora-Lynn's death and Daniel becoming the new Slave Master. Maryrose and her brother McAuthor were born on the Plantation. There father, Manchester Williamsburg, was a very hard and cruel Master, however; he had his moments when he was kind-hearted. He made sure all of his Slaves had their very own church as well as a proper pair of

shoes.The Slaves were well behaved and did very
little complaining because of his generosity. They
questioned themselves's if Daniel would follow
those same principles.
As a group of them stood in the sugarcane fields
watching the guest arrive, a female Slave spoke
out in concern,

"So do it be true? Miss Willm-burg really be's
dead?"

The Slaves ignored her and continued to work;
then another female Slave replied,

"Humph! folks say she die on count her heart wont
work no mo, po Massa Willm-burg die and it be
too much for her to bare, ya no Miss Patterson
husband be's the new massa nah!"

After hearing the comments that were made,
the Slaves had a confused look on their faces, yet
their hearts were filled with peace for a moment. In
their minds, they had been set free from the cruel
hands of Manchester Williamsburg; but there was
still a question of how Daniel would treat them.
Every Slave continued to chop sugarcane, working
themselve's harder, and pondering on the remarks
that were made by the two female Slaves. Secretly
they were praising God. It was their belief that he
allowed them to survive through the hardships of
the Plantation. Even though they were unsure of
Daniel's tactics, being able to witness a new Slave
Master somehow gave them a since of hope for a

better tomorrow, inviting a spirit of peace upon the land.

This land was the birthplace for majority of them. It overflowed with memories of beatings, killings, happiness and sorrow. It was considered hard and difficult for most Slaves to survive at Williamsburg, only a few were able to survive for decades, one of them happened to be a woman named Big Debra.

Big Debra was a heavy structured female Slave with a strong mind and personality to match. She was highly opinionated and had the power to manipulate any Slave in the Quarters. She was well respected by the others due to her longevity at Williamsburg. They honored her years of wisdom, being the Plantations' midwife, and possessing special herbs for illnesses. When she opened her mouth to speak, she was guaranteed to gain the attention of everyone in her presence.

Being in full assurance of her influence, Big Debra approached the crowd of Slaves who were gossiping. She stood with her feet flat to the ground, placed her hand on her wide hips and spoke in a hard tone, replying to the comments that were being made,

"Speck all yall know, the massa be's dead and we has a new massa nah! I may as well be the one to tellya dat dere wont be no changes made round here nah! All massa's are the same..... dey be's evil and dey has no heart fo a Slave! Sooner ya learn dat, better off ya be round here!"

The Slaves began to stop working and gathered around in a circle with Big Debra standing in the middle A female Slave by the name of Vynna began to speak out,

"Massa Patterson only has his picks on who he order round the most, he leave the rest of us lone most times."

Big Debra stood in the middle of the field; satisfied with the attention she gained from the crowd. She looked over at Vynna as if she knew nothing about her life as a Slave, then she began smiling and strutting around in a circle, speaking in a ridiculed manner,

"Massa Patterson gone order errybody round. He jus gone walk round here wit his chest stickin out all proud and say, Pick my cotton! Chop my canes! Git mo ice for my water!"

The Slaves began to laugh at Big Debra, encouraging her to continue on with her silly act. She calmed down for a few minutes and perceived a female Slave standing in the background listening. She was real quiet and shy-like. Her name was Gladdia; otherwise known as the pregnant Slave who Daniel planned to bring into his home. Instantly Big Debra decided that it would be fun to ridicule her as well; and so she did.

"We all gots tah be like Gladdie!" she said, "Run at his erry command and say: "yes massa! I gits right to it massa! Ole Massa! Massa! Massa!"

The Slaves began laughing harder at Gladdia. She done nothing but held her head down in shame. Although she spent majority of her years living on the Plantation with Big Debra and the others, she was nothing like them.Gladdia was real gentle and soft spoken. She was married to a Slave by the name of Beauford who was the complete opposite of her. She was nine months pregnant with their first child; and quietly known as Daniel's bed Slave.

Even though many of the Slaves, including Beauford, were aware of the situation involving Gladdia and Daniel; they purposely made a decision on no account to ever make mention of it. Big Debra's effort to make fun of Gladdia only reminded them of her deep secret which caused more laughter among the crowd, and more shame to Gladdia.

Everyone caused a loud disturbance on the land until a Slave by the name of Shadrach overheard them. Shadrach was a twenty-six year old field worker who was purchased by Mr. Williamsburg when he was only seven years old. He was in charge of the sugarcane bundles. It was his duty as the lead to make sure that large quantities of sugarcane were produced by the field Slaves daily. He took pride in this position appointed to him. He would spend the entire day making sure that large quantities of sugarcane were produced. Shadrach believed in hard work, if he noticed anyone slacking on their work duties, or being silly, he corrected them without any hesitation. He understood that their imprudent behavior may become a reflection on him, which could lead to punishment.

The moment Shadrach noticed Big Debra and the others being negligent and making fun of Gladdia, he approached them in the fields while carrying a load of sugarcane in his big swollen arms. He spoke out to them with authority,

"Needs to cut all dis cacklin and git back to work, massa gone have a fit if his bundles not rite round chere" he said.

Shadrach dropped the sugarcane in a huge pile. Big Debra interrupted him, speaking in a loud cocky tone. She did not care about his authority or any other Slave for that matter. Big Debra stood and leaned back with her hands on her hips; depending on her legs to help balance her heavy weight and well endowed breasts. She pointed her finger towards his face and replied in a cynical tone,

"SHADRACH! If you's do half as much work as you do walkin round here telling us what we need to be doin, we gits mo bundles done sho nuff!"
Shadrach did not spend a lot of time argueing with Big Debra, he understood that she had a strong personality and that argueing with her

would only cause more trouble. He informed the other Slaves to remain focused on their work duties and then wondered off to chop more sugarcane. As Shadrach walked away from Big Debra and the unruly group of field Slaves, Beauford came walking along minutes later, transporting more sugarcane. He unloaded it into a pile and spoke to everyone, but mainly to Big Debra,

"Whats all dis fussin bout over here?" he said, "Sounds like a buncha wile turkeys!"

Beauford looked at Big Debra with a smirk on his face, he spreaded his arms apart from one another as wide as he could, then continued speaking,

"DEBRA! You looks like one sho nuff! A big ole wile turkey!"

The other Slaves began laughing at Big Debra, this made her feel humiliated. Beauford then looked over at Gladdia, who was standing there displaying a deep smile on her face as a sign of relief. Beauford winked his right eye to assure her of his protection and loyalty and then walked away.
Beauford is the only Slave on the Plantation that can initiate Big Debra to become subdued, even though they argued on a regular basis; they loved each other as brother and sister. Together they were both separated at the age of five and sold

from the Perkins Plantation to Williamsburg; hence they possessed a very close bond that no one moreover understood.

As the field Slaves carried on with their constant routine of chopping sugarcane, making jokes and enjoying Slave quarter gossip; something unusual began to happen, something that frightened everyone in the fields. Gladdia yelled to the top of her lungs; sounding off an alarm that she is going into labor in the middle of the sugarcane fields.

Everyone discontinued what they were doing and ran quickly to Gladdia's assistance. Big Debra was the first to reach her. She placed her arms firmly around Gladdia for support. Beauford stood on the opposite side of her and attempted to assist in walking. Gladdia was in great pain. Her screams became constant every five minutes. Everyone was worried and concerned. Even though they understood the complications of delivering a baby, the loud outbursts coming from Gladdia made it impossible to consider that moment a stress-free situation.

Everyone quickly walked with Gladdia to her cabin nearby. They stood in the yard patiently while Big Debra, Ola, and Beauford were inside. As everyone waited anxiously for the baby's arrival, they could not help but wonder to themselves, if he was the one. Would this baby be something special and lead them to a better place? Whatever questions that submerged their minds would soon be discovered. The hour had arrived for another baby to be born; and deep inside, in the center of everyone's heart, they were all celebrating; they were all grateful and happy for this day.

As Gladdia layed in her bed, fighting labor pains and preparing to give birth; more and more guests were arriving at the Plantation house for Daniel and Maryrose's party. They were welcomed through the front door by well dressed house Slaves, who were serving wine and champagne on shiny silver trays. There was a male house Slave by the name of Jimmy, he was Big Debra's oldest son and Daniels most loyal servant. He was dressed in a fine tuxedo and entertained the guest by playing the piano. As everyone mingled with one another, Daniel was busy walking around from room to room, joking with other gentleman and discussing politics.

While everyone seemed to be having a good time, Maryrose found herself separated from the others and hidden in another room. As she stood there thinking about Daniel's tactics of moving a winch Slave into their home, she became disturbed and had difficulties with accepting the idea; this caused her to feel insecure.

She sat down in a chair and listened to the sounds of the guest in the other room. She stared out of a window and imagined herself being some place else, like walking in a field with beautiful flowers. In the midst of her daydream, her brother McAuthor interrupted by walking into the room sipping on a glass of wine, McAuthor was a tall, slender and handsome gentleman who considered himself a Christian man. He hardly consumed alcohol, but every now and then, he would have a glass of wine. McAuthor looked at Maryrose sitting there with a worried look on her face. His brotherly instincts made him want to grab and embrace her, yet as an alternative; he took another sip of wine and began probing for answers,

"So how you holding up sister, how you feeling?"

he asked, as he took his last sip of wine. Maryrose remained sitting in her chair and staring out the window, then she began rubbing on her swollen stomach, and taking deep breaths to relieve her anxiety; she responded effortlessly,

"A bit tired I guess, its' really been a dreadful day…..I'm worried brother, I am truly worried."

McAuthor walked closer to her and put his hands on her shoulders, he gently massaged them to help ease her of frustration; then he continued to probe,

"Whats troubling you sister, why are you worried?.....is it about the baby?"

Even though McAuthor may have disagreed with his sisters' way of doing certain things, he held a special place in his heart for her, his spirit is often unsettled when she is in pain. Maryrose

looked up at him with tears building in her eyes
and replied sadly,

"Not jus about my baby brother, its bout dat
husband of mine coming up with dat foolish idea
of moving a winch into our home to help raise our
baby!......he doesn't even care how I feel bout the
matta."

McAuthor walked toward the wall and glanced
over at a family portrait, then spoke in a confused
tone,

 "But sister, you are aware dat we both were raised
by Slaves our entire childhood, I think we turned
out jus fine….feel like dere is something more
extreme bothering you"

Maryrose slowly grabbed her stomach and rose
up from the chair. She began to walk toward the
other room in frustration. McAuthor followed
behind in an attempt to get an answer from her.
As she is walking from the room, she began to
answer with aggravation in her voice,

"Ya don't understand!....no way ya would, you
have ALWAYS taken a liking for the niggers,
even as a chile you would always run off to the
Quarters to play, eat,...ya even went to church wit
em."

As McAuthor walked behind Maryrose and
listened to her express her feelings, she turned and

faced him dead on, looking him straight in the eyes,

"Why you had rather spend more of your time with them than your own FAMILY! A disgrace you were!"

Maryrose turned her back in an attempt to walk away from McAuthor, but unexpectedly he grabbed her by the arm, swiftly turned her around to face him and spoke angrily,

"No! A disgrace is being hateful to someone who has done you no harm, treating them like there less than God's children! God is the creator of ALL things Maryrose! We are ALL created in HIS image! He does not see color, it is the heart that matters, and no one with a cruel heart can EVER live righteously…..it was cruelty that killed papa and the guilt of it all that killed mama!..you remember that sister!"

They became quiet for a moment. During the silence, they heard Daniel and the others laughing in the background. As Maryrose listened in on them, she was instantly reminded of her husbands' cruel heart, and disloyalty to her and their unborn child. She held her head down; then lifted it slowly. She looked up at McAuthor with tears building in her eyes and spoke to him in a sad tone,

"She's not jus any ole Slave from the Quarters, its Gladdie; she's his bed winch and she's with chile, her baby should be due any day now."

McAuthor looked at Maryrose with uncertainty, he was aware of Daniel spending time down in the Slave Quarters, but to be informed that it was with Gladdia, only reminded him of his brother-n-laws' unfaithfulness. Could Gladdia be carrying Daniels' baby, or is his sister overreacting as she sometimes do during situations like this. Suddenly McAuthor began filling his mind with possibilities and concerns, yet he chose not to share them with Maryrose. He wiped the tears from her eyes, took her by the arm and escorted her back to the party. They walked into the crowded room with smiles on their faces, knowing that this ordeal could be the beginning of a catastrophe. It was their intention to enjoy themselves and pretend for a moment that everything was okay.

Back in the Quarters, there were Slaves gathered around Beauford and Gladdia's cabin, some were pacing back and forth nervously, and a few of the female Slaves were standing near comforting one another as they perceive the piercing sounds of labor pains coming from the windows.

"Gladdie gon be alright?"

asked Shadrach as he sat on the cabin steps chewing on a straw.

"Having a chile be's a natural thang"

replied Vynna,

"She be jus fine!"

As everyone congregated around, praying and awaiting the arrival of the good news; Big Debra, Beauford and Ola were busy inside with Gladdia, helping and coaching her through the delivery process. Gladdia was layed prostrate in bed with her knees elevated. She was sweating, screaming and breathing hard. Although the labor pains caused Big Debra to worry, she showed no sign. She was kneeled down between Maryrose's legs, examining and coaching her through the procedure; the same as she does for anyone whose about to give birth. Beauford was busy pacing back and forth in the room, chewing on an old straw. Ola was more concerned with Gladdia's peace of mind, because of her spitituality; she stood next to Gladdia, and rubbed her forehead gently with a towel, praying silently.

"C'mon girl!…..need ya to push for me Gladdie…nah puuuuusssshhhh."
yelled Big Debra.

Gladdie was in a lot of pain. She began sweating harder and almost ran completely out of breath. She pushed; then yelled out louder,

"BIG DEBRA! somethin be wrong, somethin be wrong wit the baby! I feels it!"

Big Debra began to spread Gladdia's legs wider and looked into her vagina canal. She noticed a small foot coming out of her and discovered that the baby was attempting to come out backwards. Although this situation could be fatal and Gladdia was losing a lot of blood, Big Debra did not panic. She prepared her mind and body to perform a procedure she once had to do with another Slave who had a situation similar to this one; Big Debra began to instruct Gladdia,

"Okay nah Gladdie, I gotta do somethin to fix ya problem, gonna hurt a lil bit but I needs ya to be strong."

Big Debra looked over at Ola and Beauford and gave them an order, "Needs ya to hold her arms for me, dis may hurt her."

Beauford and Ola grabbed Gladdia's arms and continued to comfort her as she went through this hardship.

"God help me!"

cried Gladdia,

"Gimme strength for me and my baby!"

"Dontcha worry"

yelled Big Debra,

"I's fix errythang, dis baby will be jus fine Gladdie, jus hol on!"

Big Debra reached her hand inside of Gladdia's vagina and gently turned the baby around so that the baby's head was properly set for delivery; Gladdia yelled out with agony, but continued to be strong for her and her baby.

"OKAY GLADDIE! ALMOST DERE! I NEEDS YA TO PUSH GLADDIE.....PUUUUUSH!"

yelled Big Debra as she gently placed her hands in front of Gladdia's vagina to safely grab the baby's head upon delivery.

Gladdia gave two hard pushes, causing the baby to pop out in a matter of minutes. Suddenly the room filled with screeching sounds of the baby crying. Seconds later, the sound leaked through the walls and windows. The Slaves outside heard and began celebrating with one another before heading back to their duties. Although Shadrach had more work to complete in the fields, he waited patiently for Ola.

Inside the cabin, Big Debra completed the delivery process by cutting the umbilical cord with a sharp blade and wrapped the baby in soft linen,

"Oh Father God you got yaself a beautiful baby GIRL!"

cried Big Debra as she placed the baby in Gladdia's arms.

Ola began to smile, while Beauford stared from across the room with tears of joy building in his eyes. Gladdia held her new born baby close to her breasts and kissed her on the forehead. She felt as if that was the happiest moment of her life. Even though she and Beauford were expecting a baby boy, somehow she felt that God had a different plan, and he knew exactly what he was doing. Gladdia looked over at Beauford standing in the corner and softly called out to him,

"Beauford come!...come and have a look at your new baby girl."

Big Debra and Ola look over at him with anticipation. Beauford was hesitant at first because he was extremely scared of holding his baby. He looked over at Big Debra to help ease the tension; she smiled, then gave him a head nod,

"It be okay Beauford, you can do it!...go head."

Beauford slowly walked over to Gladdia. She passed him the baby. He held her closely to his chest and walked to the center of the room. He smelled her scent, felt her warmth, and tiny heartbeat. He looked down at her. Feelings of warmth and excitement overwhelm him, but all he can do was smile.

"Gonna call her Annabelle, Annabelle Louise Perkins after my great grandmama" he said proudly as he kissed her softly on the forehead,

"She will be strong like roots of an oak tree and have more than what us have." Beauford then walked over to Gladdia and layed Annabelle in her arms. He kneeled down beside the bed and watched them both, like a Lion watches his cub.

Big Debra smiled at the both of them, "Guess I's be goin nah." she said, "Got a new baby of my own I has to check on…..and I needs to do mo work in the fields before sun-down"
She looked over at Ola and made a gesture to her, "C'mon gal, you best be leavin too, fo Shadrach falls asleep on you out dere."

Ola gave Gladdia a kiss on her cheek, then followed Big Debra out the front door.

While Beauford and Gladdia enjoyed a quiet evening at home with their newborn baby girl, the late hours were fastly approaching and all of Daniel and Maryrose's guest were preparing themselves to depart the gathering. As all of them began heading toward the front door, Daniel and McAuthor were shaking hands with majority of the gentleman. Maryrose was diligently kissing each lady on the cheek. Although Maryrose produced a small amount of elegance, all the ladies treated her with a great deal of respect.

"Thankya all for coming over, please do visit our home again!"

cried Maryrose and as the last guests made their exit out the front door; a feeling of exhaustion overwhelmed everyone in the room. Daniel lit a cigar and sat on the sofa. McAuthor walked over to the bar and poured a glass of red wine. Maryrose began to assist the house Slaves in cleaning.

 "Think ima turn in for bed early" said McAuthor as he took a sip from his wine glass, "Gotta big day ahead."

   McAuthor guzzled down his wine; then walked over towards Daniel. He gave him a hand shake to wish him goodnight. McAuthor and Daniel are not the best of friends due to their differences concerning equality, nonetheless; they managed to maintain their maturity for the sake of Maryrose. Daniel responded in a gentleman like manner,

"Sleep well Author! See you in the morning." he replied as he took a few puffs from his cigar.

McAuthor walked over to Maryrose while she was cleaning and gathering up empty wine glasses. He kissed her on the cheek and wished her a goodnight as well.

"Goodnight my brother, make sure you remember breakfast with me in the morning."

Maryrose replied as she handed over a bundle of wine glasses to a servant. McAuthor informed Maryrose that he would consider their breakfast date as he walked toward the staircase. Shortly thereafter, Maryrose joined Daniel over on the sofa to allow her feet some rest. She had to ease her mind and body of the long and tiresome day.

"That reminds me!"

cried Maryrose,

"Where is dat Gladdie, I gave her exact instructions to come in from the fields and help out round here when the guest arrived!"

As McAuthor heard Maryrose's comment, he immediately turned from the staircase and spoke in Gladdia's defense,

"Saw her working hard in the sugarcane fields earlier, maybe it slipped her mind, being with-child and all."

he replied.

McAuthor had a soft heart for the Slaves on the Plantation. It was his belief that all were created equal. He would gladly risk almost anything to prevent them from being punished, killed or beatened. Maryrose made an attempt to arise from the sofa. She put her hands on Daniel's leg. He grabbed her hand tightly and assisted her in standing. She began walking and pacing the floor, instantly becoming upset with Gladdia because of her absence. She was reminded of Daniel's intentions to move her into their home. As a result; strong grudges began to develop.

 "Swear if she weren't with-chile, I would order a beating to her…..but God knows we cannot afford to lose a new born Slave due to her negligence"

 yelled Maryrose as she stood near the fireplace with her hands on her hips to support her throbbing back.
    It made Daniel feel awkward to hear Maryrose speak harmfully toward someone who he had mysteriously developed feelings for, however; he kept his feelings concealed.
    As an alternative, he made a comment and a suggestion that was more appropriate for the situation,
"You're right, be bad luck to whip a winch when she's wit-chile, could cause the infant Slave to become retarded….McAuthor, how bout ya go down to the quarters in the morning and check thangs out."

    McAuthor stood near the staircase. He was mentally prepared to answer any questions regarding Gladdia at that moment. He looked at Daniel and keenly replied;

"I will check on everything first thing in the morning."

He swiftly made his way up the staircase before any more questions transpired. He had consumed a generous amount of alcohol. He felt himself becoming intoxicated. Maryrose calmed herself long enough to make her way back over to the sofa. She sat down and thought out the situation more intensely. After a few minutes of deliberating and watching Daniel go through a second glass of Brandy, she had a clever idea,

"I shall git to the bottom of this matter right here and now!"
declared Maryrose; then she began calling for Daniel's faithful servant,

"JIMMY!....JIMMY BOY!"

she yelled,

Jimmy walked swiftly into the room and stood at Maryrose's feet awaiting her command. Jimmy was a strong house Slave, well mannered and respectful. He's been with the Plantation since birth. Daniel had a great deal of respect for him.

"Yes ma'am Miss Patterson, what can I git fo ya?"

he asked as he stood still as a brick wall and positioned his eyes to look forward.

"Hows my favorite boy doin?"

asked Daniel as he re-lit his cigar,

"Im doin jus fine massa, I's be doin jus fine."

Jimmy replied as he stood patiently awaiting a command.
Maryrose sat upright on the sofa to position herself for the conversation that was about to occur,

"Ya knows of anything happenin down in the Quarters today wit Gladdie?"

she asked;

assuming that Jimmy had all of the answers that she was looking for. Jimmy was Big Debra's son. She had a serious gossip problem. They were all convinced that Big Debra informed Jimmy of every occurrence that happened in the Quarters, so Maryrose expected immediate answers. Jimmy was hesitant at first, but then he began to explain,

"Well massa ….I uhm."

mumbled Jimmy as he began to fidget with his hands behind his back. Daniel took another puff from his half smoked cigar, then spoke aloud with firmness in his voice,

"Well if ya knows anything boy, best let us know now!"

Jimmy took a deep breath and began to explain the entire situation to the both of them,

"Well uhm, Gladdie; she be's wit'chile ya know an......well uhm my mama tells me today dat in the cane fields Gladdie start havin real bad pains in her belly, dey carries her off to the cabin and my mama helps her deliver a pretty baby gal, almost had it right dere in the fields."

Daniel instantly became nervous. He walked over to the bar and prepared another glass of Brandy. Maryrose observed his weird response but did not acknowledge it.

"You be tellin me the truth boy!"

Daniel asked anxiously as he sipped on his drink,

"Yessuh! Dey calls her Annabelle.....Annabelle be's her name suh."

Jimmy explained proudly.
Daniel and Maryrose suddenly became silent.They looked at the floor; then looked at each other. Deep inside, they both understood that there was a strong possibility of Daniel being the father

of Gladdia's newborn baby girl, but how could
they be sure of that notion?
Daniel made up in his mind right then and there
that he was going to make a special trip to the
Quarters the next morning to have a look at the
baby for himself. If indeed he was the father, he
would notice immediately. Maryrose took a deep
breath, reclined on the sofa and responded in an
uneasy tone,

"Very well Jimmy; that will be all for now, go on
and finish your chores."

Jimmy nodded his head in respect and departed
from the room.
    Maryrose sat on the sofa, rubbed her stomach
gently and pondered about what had just transpired
between the three of them. Her head began to ache
from the stress she felt building in her heart
slowly. The thing that she feared the most had
began to unfold right before her very eyes. She
looked over at Daniel standing at the bar, sipping
on another glass of Brandy and staring off into
space. Could he be experiencing the same feelings
as she? Would the secret finally unfold with an
infant running around the Plantation?
    As much as Maryrose would like to settle this
confusion with Daniel, truth of the matter is; there
wasn't any proof of him being the father of
Gladdia's baby girl. So without causing any further
commotion, she pretended as if everything was
fine and called out to him in a calm voice,

"Sweetheart, would you mind helping me up from here…I'm rather tired…think I should git to bed."

Daniel walked over and aided her in standing from the sofa. He walked back over to the bar and topped his glass off with more Brandy. Maryrose walked slowly toward the staircase holding back tears and composing her anger. Before she reached the staircase; she made a sudden stop. She turned around, looked toward Daniel; and asked him a question,

"Will you be joining me upstairs, or will your wife have to sleep alone tonight?" she asked sarcastically knowing that the chances of him coming were unlikely. Daniel continued to finish the last of his Brandy, pulled his cigar from his shirt pocket and responded in a calm voice,

"Wait for me there, I will be along shortly."

Without any argument, Maryrose turned and made her way up the staircase to the bedroom; Daniel continued to stand by the bar. He was heavily intoxicated and uneasy.

He took another sip from his Brandy and walked over to the sofa. Although his bedroom was upstairs, the guilt of him sleeping with Gladdia became too much for him to handle. Daniel reclined on the sofa and began doing some soul searching of his own, asking himself; why does he have such a weird attraction to Gladdia? What could be so special about a Slave that would cause him to be drawn to her like a magnet? Why was he jeopardizing his relationship with his wife? He knew of other Masters who enjoyed having sex with their female Slaves but that was only because they were able to force them to do un-natural things with them in bed.

Daniel had a different feeling in his heart toward Gladdia that Maryrose knew nothing about. Because of his deep feelings, he continued to creep down into the Quarters and insisted on bringing her into the Plantation house once the baby was born.

Now the questions remained; would Maryrose allow her husband to move his bed winch into their home, or would she demand that he show some respect for her and their unborn child. Seemed like the closer Maryrose got to Daniel, the further he pushed her away with his selfishness and cruelty.

As Daniel layed on the sofa with his blood stream overflowing with alcohol and his heart pounding due to stress and fear; he had a certain urge to look toward heaven and speak to God, instead; he pretended as if it all was a terrible nightmare. He eventually drifted into a deep slumber and slept until the next morning.

II

It's a quarter after six on a beautiful morning. McAuthor walked through the Slave Quarters headed to Gladdia and Beaufords cabin. He was apprehensive about the news that Jimmy delivered the night before so he found himself anxious to check on Gladdia and more importantly, see the new born baby girl. As he got closer to the cabin, he observed Beauford leaving out the front door. He had a smile on his face and appeared to be in a cheerful mood.

McAuthor approached Beauford and extended his hand to him for a handshake. He had a great deal of respect for Beauford. He was a good husband to Gladdia, very respectful, and worked hard in the fields. Beauford was aware of the high level of respect that McAuthor had for him. He opened up the conversation with a warm welcome,

"Howdy-doo! Massa Willmburg….howdy-doo dis moanin suh!"

yelled Beauford proudly as he and McAuthor approached one another outside of the cabin. McAuthor nodded his head to Beauford to show respect and then responded,

"Ahhh Beauford, a fine morning it is, I keep telling ya you don't have to call me Master when I'm in the Quarters, down here I am just McAuthor.....plain ole McAuthor."

Beauford looked at McAuthor confusingly. He didn't understand why he would prefer to be acknowledged in any other manner. He felt that any other way would be improper. Without any further hindrances, Beauford insisted on respecting him at any rate,

"Ahhh no suh!"

he replied,
"Massa would have my hide fasho if he heard me callin ya somethin otha than massa!....I has to callya dat suh, no otha way. So what can I do fo ya?"

McAuthor just smiled. He understood that Beauford wanted to respect him at any cost and did not want to take a risk of receiving a punishment. McAuthor looked at Beauford standing there, smiling and eager to go out into the fields. Somehow he became comfortable with working as a Slave. His mentality had convinced him that this was the only way of life for him and his people.That caused McAuthor to be saddened, yet he continued on with the conversation,

"Well I spoke wit Jimmy last night and word has it that you jus became a papi..that be true Beauford?"

Beauford began to smile even harder and stood with pride and dignity.

"Well yessuh! Yessuh!"

he replied excitedly, standing "flat-foot" in the dirt yard of his cabin rocking his arms back and forth,

"Was gone come an tell yall....Gladdie, well she has my baby yesterday....jus bout had her right dere in the cane fields....name be's Annabelle massa!"

As Beauford continued to brag about the new addition to his family, he was instantly reminded that Gladdia was supposed to work in the Plantation house for the gathering on the day before. His smile quickly went away and he began to plead their case to McAuthor. Beauford was aware that Maryrose was short-tempered when it involved Slaves working. He did not want his Gladdia to receive a whipping.

"Please don't be mad wit us!"
he cried out,

"Gladdie not know the baby come so soon…..I knows Miss Patterson be's mad at her on count she not show up fo the party."
McAuthor quickly puts his hand on Beauford's shoulder to calm his spirit,

"Calm down Beauford."

he instructed,

"Ya jus calm down and leave everything to me! Its gone be alright….be jus fine."

McAuthor helped Beauford to calm down,

 "You tell Gladdie I said to take good care of little Annabelle."
 he said,

"Hopes to see her soon."

    Beauford smiled in relief; then remembered a situation he perceived on the night before when he examined Annabelle. He noticed that one of her legs was slightly longer than the other, which was very disturbing. He called on McAuthor for help,

 "Massa Willmburg!, reckon ya could have a look at my babies leg, seem like one of her legs be a lil longer than the otha….though she don't seem to be in no pain, me and Gladdie worries she not be able to walk when she be of age."

McAuthor began to feel concern for the child, yet he maintained his composure to keep from worrying Beauford,

 "Be's happy to boy!"

he answered,

"But ya betta git down to the fields before Daniel finds out ya not there."

Beauford began to smile. He had complete trust in McAuthors word and was assured that everything with Annabelle would be okay,

"Yessuh!"

Beauford replied happily,

 "Yessuh massa!.....I's thankya kindly suh."

    As Beauford was making his way toward the fields for work, him and McAuthor looked out into the fields and observed Daniel heading their way on a horse. It was evident that he woke up with intentions on seeing Beauford and Gladdia's baby. As he got closer to the cabin he was surprised to find McAuthor and Beauford speaking with one another in the yard. He sat on his horse and gave them both a friendly greeting,

 "Well howdy there boys."

McAuthor looked at Danel with a strange doubtful eye, for he was aware that his greeting was an attempt to move in on him and Beauford's conversation,

"Ahhh! Good morning Dan!"

McAuthor answered in a spurious manner,

"Was jus telling Beauford here that everything is gonna be jus fine, his Gladdie jus had herself a baby gal, little Annabelle….had her round yesterday evening or so"

Beauford stood next to McAuthor with confidence and smiled proudly. Deep inside of Daniel's emotions was a jealous streak building slowly. Even though he understood that Beauford and Gladdia were married, he wanted to be the only man that made love to her. Inspite of his evil thoughts toward Beauford, he quickly jumped down from his horse and extended his hand toward him to initiate a handshake,

"Oh yes!....yes, good for you boy!"

he replied; pretending to be happy,
"Me and Maryrose got word of it jus last night, I uh….I came down here to check on you all and to see lil Annabelle."

McAuthor looked at Daniel in his eyes, he was aware that he was nervous and worried about the baby showing some sign of being his child; this caused McAuthor to become disgusted with him. Not only was he disgusted with Daniel, he had also developed compassion for Beauford. He assumed that Beauford was ignorant to the fact that little Annabelle may not be his biological daughter. To keep down confusion, McAuthor remained calm and allowed Beauford to respond to Daniel's kind gesture,

"Be Mighty pleased ya comes to see bout us suh! And Gladdie be's mighty pleased sho nuff! Well I's betta get to the cane fields suh, will dat be all suh?"

Daniel's frustration was beginning to get the best of him. He was anxious to see the baby. The conversations between him, McAuthor and Beauford were becoming lengthy and drawn out. Daniel replied to Beauford in a stern voice,

"That will due for now boy….now go on and hurry along to the fields, lots of work to be done, now git!"

Beauford smiled at the both of them and swiftly hurried along to the fields. As the two of them stood face to face with each other in the yard, McAuthor couldnt help but notice the worried look on Daniel's face. The more he stood there facing him, the more aggravated he became. The fact that Beauford was no longer around to help him suppress his feelings caused him to confront Daniel of his actions,

"So now what brings ya down to the Quarters so early in the day?"

McAuthor asked in an uncompromising manner,

"Shouldn't ya be home lookin after my sister…. instead of leaving her alone in her condition! Be a shame if she was to go into labor and you're not there near her side."

Daniel mentally positioned himself for an argument with McAuthor. He understood that McAuthor was not pleased with his behavior toward his sister. For McAuthor to observe him coming to the Quarters with the intentions of seeing Gladdia privately, was just the motivation he needed to confront him of all his foolisness. Daniel responded sharply,

"Not to worry, the house Slaves are lookin after her along wit Jimmy, besides; I need to check on Gladdie and the baby…..need her to spend more time in the home wit Mary and I….baby will be here soon and I need someone to help out for a while."

McAuthor looked at Daniel with frustration, yet he remained calm in order to get his point acrossed,

"Yes! sister mentioned that to me on yesterday."

replied McAuthor in a calm, yet aggravated tone, then he went on to say;

"But what I can't seem to understand, is why would you need more help in the home than you already have?.......mean, surely the other Slaves are capable of helping out."

Daniel began to experience the feelings of guilt, the comments made by McAuthor concerning more help in the home were convincing. Even though Daniel felt strongly that McAuthor would figure out his notions, still he felt the need to defend his decision.

"Would prefer to have someone in the home who is in the same condition as Mary."

Daniel replied,

"She will be able to nurse and care for our baby properly...Gladdie is the only one suitable for the job."

McAuthor tried hard to hold in his composure but was unsuccessful. He began to think about how often Daniel had mistreated his sister and Slaves on the Plantation. In a matter of seconds, McAuthor found himself standing face to face with Daniel and speaking in a loud tone, almost yelling,

"Suitable for my sister or suitable for YOU!......have you forgotten that Gladdie is married to Beauford and has a family of her OWN Daniel…..and what does Mary have to say bout you bringing your bed Slave into the home to raise your baby?.....As if working for you in the fields isn't enough! You're only worried about your OWN pleasuring!"

As McAuthor began to stand in Daniel's face and confront him loudly, Daniel became more upset and began to yell at McAuthor to defend himself. The two of them found themselves standing in Gladdia and Beauford's front yard argueing like two men preparing for war.

"MY WIFE IS COMPLETELY AWARE OF WHATS' GOIN ON HERE." yelled Daniel,

"YOU ARE OUTTA LINE BOY!!! PEOPLE DO THIS SORT OF THING ALL THE TIME IN THE SOUTH……NOW SHE AND I BOTH AGREE THAT HELP IS NECESSARY, AND WHILE WE STAND HERE BICKERING, OUR SLAVES NEED SUPERVISING IN THE CANE AND COTTON FIELDS BOY!"

Daniel gave McAuthor a look with his eyes suggesting that they should stop arguing with each other. McAuthor took a moment to calm down. He realized that the two of them were acting like immature children. Even though McAuthor wanted to continue pleading his case; he felt bad for disrespecting Gladdia and Beauford's home by yelling.He decided to bring the argument to a close by making a sly comment towards Daniel,

"Be not deceived, God is not mocked, for what so ever a man soweth, that shall he also reap."

McAuthor then looked Daniel deep in his eyes and walked off slowly toward the fields where the Slaves were laboring. As Daniel watched him walk away, he began to hear the sounds of a baby crying come from inside of the cabin. His heart began to beat at a steadily pace, his palms became sweaty and he could feel butterflies building up in the pit of his stomach. Without any further delaying, he began to walk toward the cabin and up the porch steps. As Daniel walked through the front door, he discovered Gladdia sitting on the edge of the bed, nursing Annabelle. Although she heard the two of them argueing, she never mentioned a word to him about it.

He looked over at her smooth dark skin, full lips and curved body and was instantly reminded of all the times he would force her to sleep with him while Maryrose was resting or Beauford was in the fields working. The thought of it all aroused him, almost tempting him to take Gladdia and force her to lie down with him right there in the cabin. He smiled, walked toward her and the baby; and began to speak in a delightful voice,

"Well now what do we have here?…….looks like we have ourselves a new addition to Williamsburg now don't we!"

Gladdia continued to nurse Annabelle, looked up at Daniel and smiled. Deep inside, she was afraid. Everytime Daniel made a visit to the Quarters, it was usually to harass or force her to sleep with him. Gladdia used her smile to hide the fear that she was feeling as she nervously rocked back and forth with Annabelle in her arms. As Gladdia reminded herself to keep smiling, and to not look Daniel in his eyes, she replied with a soft submissive voice,

"Well uhm, Massa, dis here be's my lil angel, we calls her Annabelle."

Daniel looked down at the baby girl. He carefully examined her with his eyes, paying close attention to her skin color and hair texture. He was convinced that he was not the father of the baby and suddenly became more relaxed.

"Yes I know!"

he replied excitedly,

"The news be all over the Plantation, and I must say Gladdie; what a healthy lil bundle she is."
Gladdia continued to rock Annabelle, making sure she did not look Daniel in his eyes. He may

have noticed her fear and decide to take advantage of her vulnerability.

As she concentrated on keeping herself calm, she walked over to a hand crafted cradle that Beauford spent weeks building. She positioned Annabelle there for a nap, then walked slowly over to her bed, keeping her head held down. She sat down on the end and replied nervously,

"Well yessuh, reckon so…. Beauford say somethin be wrong wit one of her legs, but I spec she grow out of it…..he be so pleased to be a papi!.....I…I know why ya come by here, I know ya be's right mad wit me for not showin up fo ya party."

Daniel looked over at Gladdia, undressing her with his eyes. She could sense him staring at her and became nervous. She continued to hold her head down, not saying a word. Silence filled the room for a few seconds; then Daniel replied to her,

"Mary was expectin ya to show up, and I know ya feels awful bout it, however; I forgive you this one time cause I got a job for ya…..real important one to me and Mary."

Gladdia lifted her head with excitement. She was happy to hear that there was a job assigned for her, and that it was not only important to him, but also important to Maryrose. It was very significant to Gladdia that she gained acceptance and approval from her because of the guilt that she felt from sleeping with Daniel for so many years. Being informed that there was a special task helped her to be more at ease about the situation.

"You and Miss Patterson has a special job for me?

Gladdia asked,

"What kinda job it be massa?"

Daniel walked over and sat down next to her. The warmth of his body heat and the smell of his aftershave made her even more nervous and uneasy. She maintained herself and remained relaxed. He put his right hand on her leg and looked into her eyes, Gladdia felt an unexplainable tingling sensation run down the spine of her back; thus she ignored the uneasy feeling and awaited his response,

"Don't want you and ya baby to return to the fields."

he said in a polite tone

,
"Something more important I have in mind, me and Mary been talking bout it, and well we decided it may be best if ya come into our home to help raise our baby once its born, you can bring Annabelle wit ya; and I can see dat you are back in the Quarters at a decent hour everyday to tend to your duties."

Gladdia became quiet for a moment. She held her head down and took a deep breath inside. It made her heart feel warm knowing that Daniel and Maryrose both wanted her in their home to help raise their newborn baby. How would her husband Beauford react to this idea? She knew that once she started spending more time in the Plantation house, Daniel would have an easier advantage toward her. He would force her to sleep with him even more than before, and this could cause problems. Gladdia lifted her head and looked him in the eye,

"Yessuh, be's mo than happy to do dat fo you and Miss Patterson suh….jus gots to talk it out wit Beauford dats all."

Daniel had already prepared himself for Gladdia to make such a response, so he rebuttled quickly,

"Already spoken with the boy, he's clear on the arrangement and thinks it a good idea. Now Gladdie I wontcha to feel right good bout this, Mary personally wants you to be at her side."

Gladdia began to smile and answered with delight,

"Well massa, I's be dere suh, ya tells Miss Patterson she can count on me to take care of her an the baby sho nuff."

Daniel rose up from the bed. He tried to hide his excitement, but had a hard time. The thought of having his bed Slave at his begging call made him feel powerful, almost like a King. He looked down at Gladdia, gave her a big smile and replied contentedly,

"Dats my gal…very good. Well I best be goin now, dere's much to be done round here today."

Daniel walked toward the front door of the cabin, Gladdia walked along with him; thanking him for stopping by to check on her and little Annabelle. As Daniel left out the front door, Gladdia turned and walked toward the cradle where Annabelle was sleeping. She looked down at her and began to cry softly. While crying, she said a prayer over Annabelle, asking God to protect her with his love and grace. Gladdia felt deep in her heart that Annabelle was a special child, sent to her to free them all from bondage; but how would she do so? How would she manage to set her people free from the hands of Daniel Patterson? Gladdia began feeling stressed. Not only did she have her daughter and a husband to look after, she also had an additional responsibility to help raise Daniel and Maryrose's new baby. The thought of it all weighed on her shoulders like a heavy bourden.

As Gladdia continued to pray over her baby and wipe the tears from her eyes, she felt a sense of peace come over her spirit assuring her that everything would be okay. She smiled to herself and reached down to pick up the cradle. She carried it to the front porch in order to keep a watch over her while enjoying the sunlight and warm breezes.

She sat on the porch, looking out at the Slaves working in the fields. She was quickly reminded that soon it would be time for her to return back to work, only this time, it would be inside of the home and under the laws of Daniel and Maryrose Patterson. The thought of it all gave her chills, yet somehow she was convinced that everything would work out for her. Gladdia knew that she had to keep God first in her life, and have faith in him to see her through those hard times.

As she sat on the porch enjoying her last days of relaxation, McAuthor was in the fields, supervising Big Debra and the other Slaves as they chopped sugarcane and carried on with gossip. Big Debra was the main instigator during the conversations. She kept everyone entertained with Slave gossip and everything going on in the main house. She was extremely nosey; always probing around the fields listening in on conversations that didn't involve her. If there was any information needed on the Plantation, it was almost a guarantee that Big Debra knew everything first hand. As she chopped sugarcane with the others, she opened up a conversation with Vynna,

"See's Massa goin over to Gladdie's jus early today, humph; he jus charge right in like a bull…..wonder what he wonts wit her, wonder

why he be over dere so early in the moanin;
Beauford not even know he was dere!"

The other Slaves ignore Big Debra, they
understood that her notions were suggesting
something that could cause confusion within the
Quarters, however; Vynna responded to her,
hoping that it would calm her down,

"Massa can go where's ever he please Big Debra,
no sense in ya questionin it, ya best hope he not
finds out what ya talkin round here gal!"

Big Debra listened to Vynna but didn't take
heed to her suggestions. She continued to entertain
her foolish thoughts by speaking more on the
subject. She stood in the middle of the sugar- cane
fields and whispers so that only a few Slaves could
hear,

"Humph, he aint neva been ova to my cabin, he
aint neva been and he aint gonna neva come
either!....you wanna know why?, cause he has no
bittness dere!.....massa know what he be cravin fo
pleasurin and it be's wit Gladdie!"

The other Slaves were shocked at the
comments that Big Debra made concerning
Gladdia. Although they all had their speculations
on what they believed was going on between her
and Daniel; no one has ever had the nerve to say
anything about it.

Vynna walked closer to Big Debra and whispered to her in a serious tone,

"Ya best to mind ya mouf fo ya git us all beat to deaf round here."

Big Debra became quiet, she was reminded of the last time she made a comment in the fields concerning Daniel and he over heard her, he beat her so badly until she walked around the plantation with a limp for weeks, thus she quickly calmed down and continued to work. None of the other Slaves mentioned anything else on the subject. While they were working diligently in the fields, Shadrach walked up carrying a bundle of sugarcane and interrupts the silence with a loud outburst,

"Hey! yall knows Gladdie not be away from the fields too much longer....massa not allow it, fresh baby or NOT!"

Everyone with the acception of Vynna remained silent. She stopped chopping sugarcane long enough to respond to Shadrach's comment,

"Yea, speck she be back out here fo too long."

Shadrach heard her comment and dropped the bundle of sugarcane in a pile with the others; and then replied,

"Did yall know that Gladdie and Beauford's lil gal has one leg dats
longer than the other? Did ya know dat?"

He said, as he stood in the middle of the field scratching the back of his head. The Slaves began to react in disbelief, Shadrach had been known in the Quarters to over exaggerate a story, and stretch the truth a little. Making a comment concerning little Annabelle's legs only proved their thoughts of him to be factual; wasn't until Big Debra stepped in and confirmed his story that the others began to believe it as valid.

"He be telling the truth."

she said boastfully,
"I help brang that lil girl to dis world and I's seen it myself.....I's not say nothin cause I know it must have been the way God tended it to be, and ya neva question God bout NOTHIN!...I jus prays dat baby make it through life dats all."

Everyone became saddened for a brief moment, their souls began to ache for little Annabelle. Each one of them said a special prayer in their hearts for her endurance on the
Plantation. Crippled or disabled Slaves had a slim chance of surviving there, in times past; they were either sold to another Plantation or beaten to death.
Before Maryrose's father died, he always believed that crippled Slaves were more of a burden than an advantage, because of this; the

Slaves vowed to always look after little Annabelle, and to teach her the ways of becoming strong and useful. The Slaves continued to work diligently in the sugarcane fields. A few of them were praying silently and singing gospel spirituals to help pass the time away.

Suddenly, the sound of the Plantation bell began to ring continuously. The sound alarmed all Slaves in the field. They were all aware that the ringing of the Plantation bell meant that either Daniel was making a big announcement, or getting ready to beat someone. They found themselves becoming nervous. Because Shadrach was in charge of the workers in the fields, he immediately took control of the situation,

"ALL RIGHT YALL"

he yelled,

"lets git a move on chere…the massa be callin and he don't like to be kept waitin."

McAuthor and all Slaves began to silently walk in a group towards the Plantation yard. As they approached the bell, they were able to notice Daniel standing near the whipping chamber displayed in the yard. Maryrose stood on the porch. They noticed Beauford standing with two other Slaves holding a whip in his hands. This caused everyone to become more anxious and nervous. They were convinced that someone was about to receive a beating, but the questions remained: whom, and why?

As the crowd made its way to the whipping chambers, Beauford began to pace back and forth nervously, as if he knew that he was about to do something that would cause him to feel ashamed. Big Debra looked at Daniel. He had a mean and cruel look in his eyes. Big Debra has seen that look before, only it was Maryrose's father who was holding the whip instead of Beauford. Big Debra's eyes filled with tears, she grabbed a hold of Vynna's hand to keep her calm. The crowd stood close to one another in terror; they looked at Daniel and awaited his announcement. Daniel looked out into the crowd, over at Beauford, then back at the crowd again. He began to speak,

"Bought yall over here cause we seem to be havin ourselves a problem, and ima get to the bottom of it. Problem is, yall niggers are spendin too much DAMN TIME lollygaggin in the fields and less time workin em......now I promise my fatha in law I would take care a dis plantation....ya see its MY job as the new overseer to make sho this land prospers. Now laz week I was almost short three dollars cause I was fifteen pounds short of sugarcane and five pounds short on COTTON!.....I know dat don't seem like much to you, but it's a whole damn lot to ME!.....I gotta soft heart for ya niggers, I don't hardly bother none of ya, but seems like I has to teach you all a lesson, ya seem to have gotten beside yaselves round here........I wont you all to work in the fields all day wit no food til I feel you have done enough!"

After hearing Daniel's speech, McAuthor instructed the Slaves to return back to the fields for work. Everyone held their heads down in shame and began walking toward the fields. All of a sudden, Daniel interrupted them and yelled out,

"HOLD ON NOW! HOLD ON!.... I DIDN'T TELL NOBODY TO GO NO WHERE."

McAuthor and the Slaves turned around and return back to where they were all standing. Daniel asked McAuthor a question,

"Author, whose in charge of the bundle amounts in the sugarcane fields?"

McAuthor knew that Shadrach was in charge of the bundles, but did not want to answer for fear of what may happen to him. McAuthor also knew that at times, Daniel could be extremely cruel to the Slaves when he was upset; he had no compassion for them. He answered Daniel calmly,

"That would be Shadrach, Daniel."

Daniel looked over at Beauford, then at Shadrach. Deep inside he had no desire to punish him, but he felt as if he needed to make an example of what would happen if the Slaves continued to slack in their work duties. Daniel called out to Shadrach in a sharp tone,

"Shadrach, come here boy!"

Shadrach walked up with a worried look in his eyes. He was so nervous inside until he found himself on the brink of urinating on himself. He figured out Daniel's intentions on giving him a beating, and what's worst is that Daniel intended to force Beauford to carry out the task. This act counted as a disgrace to them both. Shadrach looked to Beauford as a father figure. He immediately began to apologize to Daniel,

"Massa I's be awful sorry suh.....I wont allow it to happen again!"

Daniel showed no concern for Shadrach's defense, instead he ordered him to take his shirt off. Shadrach was hesitant at first; but gradually obeyed Daniel's commands. He wanted to ensure that his beating wouldn't become more severe. Shadrach began crying softly as he took his shirt off. His knees were trembling and his heart was beating with fear. All he could think about was the pain that would attack his back from one lash of the whip. His blood pressure arose so high until he began to feel light headed, and could no longer hide his emotions. He began to cry out,

"Massa...oh massa please have mercy on me massa."

Daniel heard Shadrach's cry for mercy, but ignored him. He looked over at the two male Slaves and instructed them to cuff him to the whipping chamber. McAuthor and the other Slaves stood there looking terrified as they witness him hanging from the chamber with tears flowing from his eyes. Daniel looked over at Beauford and gave him a command,

"Aww right Beauford, when I give you the word, I want you to begin."

Tears formed in Beauford's eyes. He couldnt believe that he was faced with having to do something so cruel and evil; what was worst is that he had to be this way toward someone who he considered to be a brother.

Beauford's hand began to tremble. He felt sickly in his stomach. All he could think about was his little girl and how one day she may have to witness this same act. He became short of breath from the emotions inside, yet he grew enough courage to speak against the cruel punishment,

"Massa I can't."

he said sadly with tremble in his voice,

"Shadrach be's like a lil brotha to me….jus cant do it massa….jus cant!"

Daniel instantly developed a feeling of strength and dominance. He was in control of all Slaves. They were all at the mercy of his voice. Every command made him feel more powerful and vigorous. He looked at Beauford with evil and wickedness in his eyes and replied maliciously,

"You will do it...or you will be next... it's your choice!"

McAuthor looked at Daniel and the evil in his eyes. He was afraid for Shadrach, so afraid until he wanted to do all that he could to prevent him from being beaten. He looked around at the others. He saw the hurt in their eyes. He felt the energy of their fear. The silent cries that he heard from them made him want to chain Daniel to a whipping chamber and give him a dose of what it felt like to be treated like an animal. McAuthor jumped down from his horse, stepped forward and yelled out belligerently,
"Daniel, I will personally make sure all the bundles are done, if I have to work them all night."

Big Debra stood there listening with her feet planted solid to the ground. She held Vynna and Shadrach's wife, Ola by the hands with a firm grip. She used her big burly shape as a strong tower to help them feel more protected. Because of McAuthors willingness to save Shadrach, a spirit of courage formed on the inside of her heart. She opened her mouth, fell down on her knees, raised her hands toward Daniel and began to cry out,

"Pleeeeeeease Massa!.....pulllllllease have mercy on em'…I's take the whipping massa, lemme take it!"

Her voice was so strong and powerful until it rung throughout the entire Plantation. Daniel interrupted Big Debra swiftly,

"Enough!.. Big Debra you are way outta line for this, and YOU Author, always goin out your way for the niggers! I will have order…..this isn't your matter!"

Shadrach hung there in the whipping chamber with his shirt off. His head hung down in shame and his sweat formed a puddle in the dirt. Big Debra remained on her knees crying and Beauford stood in unbelief, holding the whip in his hands. Maryrose was so nervous. She took one last look at Shadrach, then walked into the house; closing the door behind her.
Daniel looked at Shadrach, then over at Beauford and yelled out,

"NOW BEAUFORD!"

Tears fell heavily from Beauford's eyes as he began to hit Shadrach across the back with the whip. Shadrach screamed out with agony. Every Slave that was watching began to feel Shadrach's cry rip through their hearts like a sword. One lash from the whip caused an opening of his skin.

Knowing that Ola had to witness this spiteful act of brutality caused him even more pain.

Shadrach cried out to God for mercy. The seeping of the sweat going into his open wounds prolonged the torture even longer. Daniel yelled out the word:

"AGAIN!"

Beauford began to cry harder as he struck Shadrach across his back once more, ripping more skin from him and causing more excruciating pain. Shadrach cried out even louder as Daniel commanded Beauford to strike him with the whip continuously.

By the sixth lash of the whip, Shadrach's back was covered with blood. The whip tore into his back like sharp blades causing his body to go into shock. His heart rate slowed down. His eyes roll in the back of his head. He passed all bodily fluids through his trousers and onto the ground.

His screams were so thunderous until Gladdia heard them as she sat in the cabin nursing Annabelle. It was if the sounds echoed from her walls and roof top. As Gladdia sat there on the edge of the bed, listening to the sounds of Shadrach being whipped; she became saddened and afraid. She held her baby close to her breast and began rocking back and forth.

She asked herself, what did this poor Slave do to deserve such a bad punishment? Was he disobedient, was he dishonest, or was he just a plain old Slave being used as an example for cruelty. Gladdia rose up from the bed with

Annabelle in her arms. She walked toward the cradle and placed her there to rest. As tears fell slowly from her eyes, she looked down at her baby Annabelle and began to pray,

"Oh God, please save my child from this evil place, help her to find her way; please protect her, don't let no harm come to her; in Jesus name, amen".

Meanwhile, back at the whipping chamber, Beauford was ordered to give Shadrach a final lash across his back. He was barely alive and breathing. His eyes were overflowed with tears from hurt, anger, and shame. The two Slaves standing aside began unlocking him from the chamber. As saliva and blood streamed slowly from his mouth, he fell to the ground like a heavy sack of potatoes. His face was buried in the dirt.

Big Debra and Ola ran swiftly to aid him in standing. He was much too weak. Beauford held his head down and looked over at Shadrach laying there with Big Debra and Ola surrounding him. He instantly became more upset and frustrated with the situation. He was upset with Daniel, and also upset with God. Why would he allow such awful things to happen to him and his people? Why would he give white people so much authority over them? Why would the God that he was always taught to place high above everything put him in this kind of predicament?

Beauford had no answers, all he could think of was how blessed he must have been to have his wife and baby girl back at the cabin waiting for him. With more tears building in his eyes, he allowed the whip to fall from his hands unto the ground. He began running as fast as he could toward the Slave Quarters; never looking back.

With sweat running into his eyes and heart pounding at a rapid speed, he ran the entire way to his cabin. He ran up the steps and through the front door. He found Gladdia rocking the cradle with Annabelle inside; laying peacefully.

He looked down at his daughter and felt his inner strength fabricating. He picked her up from the cradle, held her close to his chest and began pacing the floor. Tears streamed slowly from his eyes. Gladdia took one look at him and a feeling of sympathy flooded her soul. She wanted to instantly grab him and hold him tightly in her arms. She wanted to tell him that everything would be ok, but she was not convinced. She looked over at him holding their daughter in his arms. She took a deep breath, pulled her ragged gown close to her breasts and quietly asked him,

"Who's dey beat out dere?"

Beauford stopped pacing the floor and stood in a corner of the room. He rocked Annabelle gently in his arms and responded with anger,

"Shadrach!.....he made me beat Shadrach Gladdie!....never known a man to be so evil....Massa Willmburg not even do dat!!!"

Gladdia walked over and sat on the edge of the bed,

"What he make you do the beating fo?"

she asked in a confused voice,

"You not be the massa! You jus a Slave like he is."

Beauford gave Annabelle a kiss on her forehead and continued to rock her gently, then responded,

"Cause I tells ya he be the DEVIL Gladdie!....be's the devil himself!"

Beauford walked over to position Annabelle in her cradle. He looked down at her and rubbed her tiny legs. He was instantly reminded of her birth defect. He was also reminded that it could be serious and cause her to be crippled for life. Beauford became more worried for her. He looked over at Gladdia and continued to express his feelings, but with more emotion,

"Gots to be something better for us and our daughter Gladdie... hearing dat boy scream like dat ripped my heart apart I tell ya!....like I's beatin my own kin, it tore my heart to shreds Gladdie....to SHREDS!"

As Beauford expressed himself to Gladdia, there was an unexpected knock at the front door; a constant knock. Gladdia looked over at Beauford and became scared. Beauford grabbed his rifle from the corner of the room and walked toward the front door. When he opened the door, Big Debra was standing there. She was crying and appeared to be highly upset. She did not greet Beauford; she ran past him and into the bedroom. She hugged Gladdia tightly and sat down beside her to speak out in anguish,

"Gladdie....what us gone do round here?...Massa be down right evil for what he did!"

Big Debra was extremely disturbed and petrified. She could hardly think clearly. She sat there nervously on the bed and used the bottom of her dress to gently wipe the tears from her eyes and the mucus from her nose. She spoke to Gladdia with great concern in her voice,

"Gladdie....oh Gladdie what us gone do round here?.....Massa be's down right evil fo what he did to Shadrach!"

Gladdie sat there on the bed next to Big Debra and look saddened. She glanced over at Beauford, who was still looking shook up from the beating that he gave to Shadrach. She held her head down with her arms folded in her lap and replied with a soft, yet strong tone,

"I knows it....I knows it all to well, the devil can only be what he was created to be, and the massa….he gots the devil in em' dats why he do bad thangs to us."

Big Debra felt something rise on the inside of her; a feeling of anger. She rose from the bed and began pacing the floor. Her strong weight and heavy feet caused the weak floor boards to screech. She continued walking as if she was light as a feather,

"It aint right I tell ya!" she bellowed, "just aint right!"

Gladdia listened to Big Debra and looked away. She wanted to tell her and Beauford about the visit she had from Daniel earlier, but she was too ashamed. Gladdia knew that Beauford and Big Debra would worry for her once they found out that she would be Daniel's new house Slave. She realized that she had no other option. The problem was eating her up inside to the point of making her feel sick. Without any more thought, she held her head down and stared at the floor boards. She began telling them both the story of what happened,

"He come by here dis moaning jus afta ya left here Beauford…..he tell me he wants me to work in the house and help raise dey baby….I….I…not wanna go! Not want Anna round dat evil, but he say Miss Patterson be needin me,….he say she the one who ask fo me!"

Big Debra ran over to Gladdia and stood in front of her. She leaned over and looked at her face to face,

"We has no choice in the matta round here."

she said,

"He got all the power, we has to do whateva he tells us to do. Eitha we do it, or what happen to Shadrach happen to US!...may even worst."

Beauford stood at the entrance of the bedroom. He pretended to be in shock over the announcement, but was already aware of the arrangement since earlier that day. When Daniel stopped by to visit Gladdia, Beauford became very skeptical. As the two of them were talking in the cabin, Beauford stood outside of the bedroom window and eavesdropped on the entire conversation. Although he was bold and intelligent enough to do something so crafty, he could not build up the courage to tell her what he did. He held on to his secret and walked over to her. He sat down on the bed and grabbed her by the arms

.

"Dat man put his hands on you or my baby I's kill em."

He said in full assurance,

"Let dem take my life for I allow him to keep hurting you, YA HEAR ME WOMAN!"

Beauford remembered hearing the comment that Daniel made to Gladdia earlier about it being Maryrose who wanted her in the home. He became more furious. He knew that Daniel was lieing. He stood up from the bed and walked toward the entrance of the room,

"White woman done no sucha thang!"

he mumbled,

"She be knowing what massa do down here in the Quarters.....I heard errythang!"

he said,

"I stood out dere, and I hears everythang outside dat window and I tell ya Gladdie!....he has one thang on his mind and I gots a real bad feelin bout it!"

Gladdia looked over at Beauford in shock. She could not believe that her husband was listening in on her and Daniel's conversation. Even though she was not upset about the situation; the thought of it all made her feel as if Beauford had a trust issue with her. Those feelings made her uneasy. Gladdia wanted to question Beauford of his deviousness, but before she had an opportunity to do so, they were all interrupted by yelling coming from outside of the cabin; it was Shadrach's wife Ola.

"BIG DEBRA!....BIG DEBRA!!....COME QUICK!"

she yelled as she stood in Beauford and Gladdia's front yard. The three of them went running out of the cabin door and stood on the front porch. They were all afraid and in a panic state of mind. They had already witnessed a cruel punishment being done to poor Shadrach. Ola's screaming and yelling made them all nervous again. Gladdia stood there wondering if things could get any worst. Beauford stepped out in front of them,

"Whats the matta witcha gal!"

he yelled.

Ola stood still long enough to catch her breath and gather her thoughts, she replied frantically,

"MISS PATTERSON…HER BABY COMIN AND SHE NEEDS YA BIG DEBRA…..YA GOTS TO COME NOW!!!"

Big Debra immediately cleared the situation about Shadrach out of her mind and concentrated on the matter that was at hand. She ran off the porch. Ola grabbed her hand and they both ran toward the Plantation house.

As Beauford and Gladdia both stood on the porch and Ola and Big Debra ran toward the house, the spirit of depression began to attack there minds. They both realized that the time had finally came for Daniel and Maryrose baby to be born, this meant that Gladdia would be spending more time in the Plantation home, and less time with Beauford. Daniel would have more free-will with Gladdia. She would be there to obey his every command. This type of arrangement caused Beauford to worry and question; what would happen to their family at that point?

When Big Debra and Ola arrived at the Plantation house, they ran as fast as they could upstairs to Daniel and Maryrose's bedroom. When they walked into the room, they found McAuthor and Daniel pacing the floor. They discovered Hattie, a field Slave standing near Maryrose as she layed prostrate in bed holding her stomach and breathing hard. Ola quickly grabbed her right hand, Hattie grabbed the other and Big Debra spreaded her legs apart to examine the baby's delivery process. Maryrose had been experiencing labor pains for over an hour now and had become impatient. She began to breath harder and yelled out to Big Debra,

"HOW MUCH LONGER!....HOW MUCH LONGER!"

Big Debra placed her four fingers into Maryrose's birth canal and felt the babies head at the surface,

 "Wont be long now ma'am..not long at all!"

she said in comfort, to help Maryrose relax more,

"Just need ya to keep on breathing and give me a big ole push ma'am!.........now puuuuuuuush! Miss Patterson puuuuuuuuuuuuush!...puuuuuuuuuuuuuush!"

 yelled Big Debra as she continued to coach her through the delivering
process.

Maryrose pushed and pushed as Big Debra gave her the instructions and in less than three minutes, the sounds of a baby squealing begin to ricochet from the bedroom walls. McAuthor and Daniel looked over at the baby from across the room and began to smile. All of the Slaves were delighted to see a new addition to the Plantation. Daniel swiftly walked over and sat close to Maryrose. Big Debra smiled at the both of them, she layed the baby in Maryrose's arms and said proudly,

"Good lawd done bless ya wit a baby boy!"

Daniel began to play with the baby's hands and feet. Maryrose held him close to her breast and smiled as she kissed him on the forehead. After a few minutes of contemplating on what to name him, Maryrose made an announcement that was loud enough for everyone in the bedroom to hear,

"He's so beautiful....so perfect, think we's call him Jamison; Jamison Daniel Patterson."

Everyone in the room took a moment and glanced down at him; then they all looked up and smile. Oddly everyone agreed that the name fit him perfectly.

III

Five months later; Maryrose is walking and prancing through the house giving orders and sippin on a glass of red wine. She always gave the house Slaves a large number of instructions and cleaning duties to complete daily, however Gladdie had more responsibilities than others,
 "Okay Gladdia, afta ya done nursing the children, wontcha to dust the furniture, mop the dining room floor and help git dinner started."

Maryrose would say to her as she would unpleasantly demand all these duties just before leaving the house. Often times, Gladdia would become frustrated, yet without complaining, she would sit in her chair, breast feed both children, and sing gospel spirituals to herself softly. Maryrose was very unkind to Gladdia in regards to the children. She always insisted that during feeding time, Jamison would be considered first, then Annabelle. She was also very neglectful; she never nursed her son, changed his diapers, or tucked him into bed at night. Gladdia was responsible for all of those duties.

Although Maryrose wasn't as hard on the Slaves as Daniel, she enjoyed giving house orders to all of them. It made her feel as if she had authority when Daniel was away. The Slaves all respected her. No matter how frustrated they would become, they would all nod their heads after every command and say, "yes ma'am, "no ma'am" and "I gits right to it ma'am."

Doing work duties in the home didn't trouble Gladdia as much as it did the others. She was blessed to be surrounded by two beautiful babies who constantly kept a smile on her face. Sometimes she would find herself playing with them for hours; talking to them, tickling them, and playing games like "peek-a-boo." Often times she would find herself looking forward to getting up each morning and taking care of them. Her days in the home were pleasant, except for the days when Daniel would take advantage of her by being abusive and forcing her to have sexual interaction with him. These vicious acts transpired at least twice a month.

Taking care of the babies and doing her work duties became second nature to Gladdia, with the exception of the other house Slaves; she had a lot of privacy, which came in handy on those days when she spent quality time talking to God. McAuthor would hang around the house from time to time and discuss with them spirituality and inspirational thoughts. The house Slaves enjoyed these times with him because it gave them all a sense of encouragement. Some of them found it hard to believe that a Caucasian man could be capable of being so kind and pleasant to them. Big Debra convinced them all that his reason for being so kind was because he had a sexual attraction to the female Slaves, and secretly admired the strength of the male Slaves. Contrary to what they all believed, McAuthor was a man of God who desired to become a Minister. It was his belief that all men were created from the same God, and that no man is greater than the other.

Big Debra had plenty to say about everything on the Plantation. Even though most of her stories were exaggeration or partly true, the other Slaves had a great deal of respect for her. They considered her words to be accurate. All of the Slaves enjoyed Big Debra's gossip; it helped the time in the fields pass quicker. She would walk around the fields most times with her baby Eliza strapped to her back, and speak to the crowd as if she were a public speaker making an announcement.

Although Gladdia enjoyed being in the house with little Jamison and Annabelle, she missed being in the fields, listening to Big Debra and laughing with the others. But no one missed Gladdia working in the fields more than her husband Beauford, who was against the whole idea of her working in the house from the very beginning. He hardly had any quality time with her. The thought of Daniel taking advantage of

Gladdia created a lot of arguments between the two of them. One main concern was his little girl Annabelle. Beauford often pondered on the thought of Daniel being her biological father.

Even though he was convinced that Gladdia loved him dearly; he could not get beyond the fact that she was forced to have sex with Daniel throughout there entire marriage. These thoughts haunted him constantly, especially during work. One late evening in the fields, Beauford found himself missing his wife and daughter more than ususal.The disturbing thoughts in his mind concerning Daniel and Gladdia caused him to become upset, leading him to become nonchalant about being punished or breaking Plantation rules. Beauford felt that he had a right to see his family at any given time. One evening he made a decision to go to the Plantation house after work and demand to see his wife and daughter.

Once the moment arrived for him to leave the fields, he did exactly what his mind instructed him to do.Without thinking twice, he ran as fast as he could for the home of Daniel and Maryrose. As he was running through the fields, his mind was filled with fearful thoughts. Beauford knew that he was not allowed to visit the Plantation home without permission, but he needed to see his wife and daughter.

He needed to look into his wife's eyes and embrace his daughter in his arms. He felt deep in his heart that if he could only make his way to the house and see the both of them for only a few minutes; his heart would be at ease, and he could

ignore the disturbing thoughts that haunted his
mind on a daily basis.
Beauford ran as fast as he could through the fields
until he reached the Plantation house. Without
hesitation, he began knocking on the front door.
He knocked several times until Jimmy answered.

"What can I do for you Beauford?"

asked Jimmy as he stood in the doorway blocking
the view.
Beauford became nervous, he was aware that
Jimmy was a loyal servant to the Patterson's and
followed every order accordingly, so this visitation
would not be an easy one,

. "Jimmy, I was wantin to speak wit the massa."

Beauford mumbled in a low tone,

"Haven't seen Gladdie or the baby all day, I wanna
know if I be able to see em, dats all."

Jimmy stared at Beauford for a few seconds,
deep inside he wanted to open the door and allow
him to see his wife and daughter. Because of his
loyalty to Daniel and his fear of receiving a bad
punishment, he was forced to not be cooperative
with him. He tried to send him away from the
house without causing any confusion.
"Gladdie, she be busy right now with the babies
and preparing supper, I let her know ya stop by."

Jimmy replied with an unyielding voice, as his eyes looked downward.

Jimmy attempted to send Beauford away by closing the door in his face. Beauford grabbed the door and continued to speak, this time in a much louder tone,

"Jimmy, I has to see my Gladdie and lil girl….jus needs to know if dey be's alright, can ya let the massa know I's be here to check on em?"

Jimmy was disturbed by Beaufords' relentless behavior; however he understood his stance in this situation. As a result, instead of yelling at him; he spoke to him in a low, yet forceful tone, which suggested that he left immediately before trouble began,

"Toldya Gladdie be real busy right nah!"

he replied,

"I will tell her that you stopped by… now go on before you get yourself in a heap a trouble….go on nah!"

Jimmy and Beauford look at each other. Jimmy's eyes insinuate that there was something peculiar going on with Gladdia. Beauford interpreted that hidden message and became angry. Suddenly he heard crying coming from inside. He instantly recognized the tone.

"DATS MY ANNABELLE!!"

he cried out, pushing Jimmy from the door and rushing into the sitting area of the house.

Beauford pushed Jimmy so hard until he almost fell to the floor. He yelled out for Beauford to stop but he did not listen. He ran over to Annabelle as she layed next to Jamison on a soft blanket. He picked her up and began to rock her gently in his arms until the crying stopped. Jimmy stood in the doorway of the room, watching Beauford hold his daughter as if he wanted to protect her from harm. In that moment, Jimmy felt a since of love enter the room, he thought to himself how difficult his life must have been, wanting to see his family and not being able to.

Jimmy was afraid for Beauford. He was aware that Daniel was upstairs and if Beauford was caught in the house without permission, it could result in extra work in the fields or a beating. He decided to give him one last warning, but before he could suggest anything, Daniel and Gladdia walk down the staircase together, one behind the other with Daniel leading.
Beauford looked upward at the two of them as he held Annabelle in his arms. He was reminded of why he worried so deeply for his family.

Although he was upset at what he saw, Beauford understood that Daniel was in control over their lives. He would always be able to do whatever he wanted to Gladdia. There wasn't anything he could do to stop him, his voice or opinion had no value. Gladdia walked down the staircase behind Daniel, she looked down and saw Beauford standing there. She looked into his eyes; then quickly held her head down. She was ashamed.

As the two of them reached the bottom of the staircase, Gladdia stood to the side with her hands behind her back, head held down and body trembling with fear for the unknown. Jimmy spoke to Daniel to show respect, then immediately tried to explain the situation at hand. Daniel just pretended as if he said anything at all, in fact; he ignored Jimmy, then spoke out to Beauford in a harsh one,

"What are ya doin here boy! Shouldn't ya be out in the fields workin!"

Beauford became nervous, however; the presence of his baby helped to calm his nerves well enough to respond without his voice trembling, he spoke to Daniel like a strong black man,

"Ahhh yessuh, massa...I.....I wanted to know if I could see Gladdie and my baby suh, jus wanna look at em suh."

"You will have plenty a time to LOOK at em when her work is done HERE!"

replied Daniel,
"For now you return back to the fields and don't ever come back less I send for ya, or you will be severely punished. Am I clear on that BOY!"

Beauford took a deep breath, looked over at
Gladdia, then at Jimmy. He kissed Annabelle on
her forehead and responded in a strong humbled
voice,

"Yes suh, wont happen again suh!"

Daniel looked over at Gladdia and Jimmy, then
over at Beauford; then he replied,

"Very well boy, now hurry along before I get
ANGRY!"

Beauford took another look at Gladdia. She
nodded her head at him to help ease his mind. He
walked over and positioned Annabelle back on the
blanket next to Jamison, then quickly left out the
front door. Daniel watched Beauford leave the
room, then walked over to Gladdia and stood face
to face with her; he asked her a question in a rough
tone, almost yelling,

"Did you send for him gal!"

Gladdia heard the sound of his loud voice, but
chose to hold her head down and not answer.
Jimmy became nervous to the point of shaking, but
he did not interrupt. Daniel repeated his question
to Gladdia; only this time speaking louder and
more rough,

"DID YOU SEND FOR HIM!"

Daniel's tone was so loud and forceful until it frightened the babies and they begin to cry out. Gladdia's heart began to beat at a rapid speed, she started crying as well. Gladdia had been working for Daniel long enough to know when he was highly upset with her, so she responded in a low submissive tone,

"No massa."

She replied fearfully,
"I not send for em', I swear to it!"

Daniel knew that Gladdia was telling the truth. She had too much respect for him to intentionally tell a lie. He walked over toward Jimmy, leaving her to attend to the children. Jimmy was standing near the entrance way of the room with his head held down. He realized that he was in trouble, but at what degree? Daniel asked Jimmy a questioned, a question that caused Jimmy's stomach to become upset from anxiety.

"You deliberately disobeyed me boy?....LOOK AT ME!"

Daniel asked as he stood close to Jimmy.
Jimmy held his head up high and looked Daniel in his eyes. Even though he was extremely afraid, he swallowed the lump building in his throat and replied with a clear tone,

"Tries to stop him massa….tries to stop him from coming in suh!"

Daniel heard Jimmy's response and became silent. At that moment Jimmy's blood rushed through his veins, his heart started pounding and sweat ran from the peak of his forehead into his eyes. His mind instructed him to take a deep breath to calm his nerves, but before opportunity presented itself; Daniel severely slapped him across his warm face with the palm of his hand, causing his mouth to bleed.

He stood in front of Jimmy with his right hand burning, he used that same hand to lift Jimmy's chin to witness the tears flowing from his eyes. He looked over at Gladdia, then back at Jimmy and said with great authority,

"Next time try harder boy!"

Jimmy locked his knees to control his tremble, wiped the tears from his eyes and took a deep breath to ease his mind of the embarrassment and shame; then he responded to Daniel in a calm tone,

"Yes master as you wish suh!"

As Daniel walked away triumphantly toward the dining area, he turned around to face Gladdia. She was kneeled down on the floor, comforting the babies.

"Make sure dinner is ready soon."

He commanded her,

"Maryrose doesn't like waiting."

After making his decree to Gladdia, he did not give her a chance to respond. He walked from the room, leaving the two of them alone with the children.

Gladdia and Jimmy found themselves in a small state of depression as they both felt remorseful for one another. Gladdia took a look upon the innocent faces of Annabelle and Jamison, as she gently rubbed there backs to comfort them. She realized that hate wasn't something that babies were born with; it's something that is taught when they are older by hateful people. Even though Gladdia was raised to never hate anyone; it was her deepest prayer that Annabelle and Jamison could grow up in a world that was different from the one her and Jimmy were forced to live in; a world that would allow them both to love freely.

Later on that evening, Gladdia completed all of her work in the house and headed home with Annabelle to see her Beauford. As the both of them walked through the Quarters, she was reminded of the situation that occurred earlier. Even though she recognized her husbands' reason for wanting to see her and the baby, she couldn't quite understand why he would go against the laws of the Plantation. In her mind, Beauford knew everything about her and Daniel. Why would he put himself in harms way? Doesn't he understand how much she and Annabelle rely on him for their strength?

The more she thought of the situation, the more upset she became. A strange feeling grew on the inside of Gladdia's stomach. She knew that once she reached the cabin and walked through the door, that Beauford would be their waiting with his mind overflowing with malicious thoughts and she would have to provide an explanation. Gladdia tried to prolong the confrontation with her and her husband by walking slower and taking her time through the grassy fields; but the slower she walked, the quicker her cabin appeared. Gladdia slowly walked into the cabin with Annabelle. They walked into the bedroom and found that Beauford was not there. This gave her a sense of relief. As she situated Annabelle into the cradle, she began to pace the floors and sing a gospel hymn to help calm her nerves. Seconds later, Beauford walked into the cabin, slamming the door behind him.

Gladdia left Annabelle in the cradle and walked toward the wood oven stove to heat up some left over soup. Beauford began pacing the floor. Gladdia pretended as if everything between them were okay by greeting him warmly,

"Glad you're home, spose I go ahead and get ya supper started."

Gladdia said as she began to put wood in the
stove. Beauford walked toward the bed. He sat
down as if he were frustrated. He replied back to
her in a loud tone,

"NOT BE HUNGRY....I'S NOT BE HUNGRY
AT ALL!"

Gladdia continued to speak warmly toward him,
ignoring the fact that he was frustrated,

"Beauford ya needs some food in ya belly.... out
there workin all day in the fields."

Beauford heard Gladdia's response and became
more aggravated. He stood up from the bed and
began yelling at Gladdia. He yelled so loud until it
disturbed Annabelle and she began to cry. The
sounds coming from Annabelle crying and
Beauford's yelling caused Gladdia to become more
upset. She could no longer pretend as if everything
were okay. She slammed the pot down on the stove
and walked toward Beauford; looking him straight
in his eyes and yelled,

"WELL I SPOSE YA JUS GON STARVE
YOSELF TO DEATH AINT YA!! AND YOU
CAN YELL AS LOUD AS YOU
PLEASE!!!...IT'S NOT GONNA CHANGE
ANYTHANG ROUND HERE!!"
Once Beauford heard Gladdia yelling at him,
he humbled himself. It broke his heart to see his
wife upset. Beauford sat down on the edge of the

bed, held his head down; his eyes looked down at the floor,

"Well I spose if I die off…wont have to see what be happenin to my wife and baby girl now would I…."

he said.

Gladdia heard Beauford's response, walked over and grabbed Annabelle from the cradle. She began to rock her to stop the crying. She looked down at Beauford and saw the hurt on his face. She walked closer to the bed where he sat there, looking depressed.

She stood looking down at him and rocking Annabelle in her arms. Beauford continued to look down at the floors, his heart felt heavy. He swore for years that he would never mention anything about her and Daniel, but only keep it hidden in his heart and mind. Now he felt as if he had no other choice. He had to get it off his heart before it killed him. Beauford looked up at Gladdia standing in front of him holding his baby girl. He wiped the tears from his eyes and began to pour his heart out to her,

"Think I's be dumb Gladdie? Think I not know what the massa be doin to ya when I's not around? I knows why he make ya work at the house all day long!"

Beauford held his head down to allow the tears in his eyes to flow freely to the wooden floors; he continued to explain,

"I knows Gladdie! I know what he done and what he been doin, errybody round here knows bout it! Dey know he take the one thing meant for only me and he do's what he wonts wit it. All the love you has inside for jus me, he take it all from you! He jus keep takin til one day aint nothin left Gladdie, aint nothin left for me! what I's spose to do wit my love, the love I have fo ya Gladdie? He wont lemme love you know mo!"

Gladdia walked closer to Beauford, layed Annabelle in his arms. He held her close to his chest and gently rubbed her head. Gladdia kneeled down between Beaufords' knees and began to cry out to him silently,

 "Only til the baby grows old, then he lemme go Beauford, he lemme come back to the fields witcha."

    Beauford looked at Gladdie in disbelief and continued to hold Annabelle in his arms. His frustration inside was forcing him to yell out to her, but instead he replied in a low tone, being extra careful to not disturb the baby,

"You be's my wife!"

he retorted,

"But you belongs to the massa, you not belongs to me Gladdie! We all belongs to the massa til we die!"

Gladdia listened to Beauford cry out to her. Secretly she believed every word but had persuaded herself to believe that somehow things would get better. She looked him deeply in his eyes and replied softly,

"Not be true Beauford, that not be true."

Even though Gladdia spoke it from her mouth, she was not convinced that she believed it anymore. She looked at Annabelle resting in Beauford's arms and gazed into her eyes. She saw nothing but a beautiful representation of what God had blessed them to create together. Gladdia then looked into Beauford's teary eyes and said to him,

"See Beauford, we belongs to YOU! Me and the baby, we all belongs to you Beauford, ya always remember dat."

"Part a me wonts to believe it Gladdie."

Beauford replied,

"But I have a bad feeling the good lawd send her to us, but she not be mine, and you not be mine either. I......I gots nothin Gladdie, gots nothin! I rather die Gladdie! Rather die right here on dis

Plantation den feel dis pain I's be feelin….dis pain here not meant fo no man to feel."

Gladdia looked up at Beauford; then rose up from the floor. She walked toward the empty cradle and began to cry softly. Beauford held Annabelle tightly in his arms, stood up and walked outside to the porch to look at the stars. Gladdia watched him as he left the room. Moments later, she walked over to the bed, crawled in slowly and layed in a fetal position. She cried herself to sleep.

While Beauford sat out on the porch, looking at the stars and playing with Annabelle, he heard horses in the distance. He looked ahead and saw what appeared to be Daniel and two of his friends coming towards the cabin riding horses. Beauford became slightly worried; Daniel had visited them often, but never at late hours. As Daniel and the two gentlemen moved in closer to him, Beauford held Annabelle securely to his chest.

Daniel and his friends arrived to the cabin and sat on there horses out front. It was obvious by their behavior that they had been drinking alcohol. By Beauford knowing that Gladdia was inside sound asleep helped him to feel more secure. Although he could sense trouble in the air, Beauford kept calm and gave Daniel a friendly greeting,

"Howdy massa, mighty late of ya to come visit, anything I's can do fo ya?"

he said.

Daniel looked at his two friends and they all began to laugh at Beauford teasingly. Daniel climbed down from the horse and walked toward Beauford,

"May wanna take little Annabelle inside for a moment."

he said.

"We goin for a little late night ride Beauford, wontcha to come out wit us."

Beauford looked at the three of them in his yard. Deep in his heart he knew that Daniel had a wicked plan in mind. He tried to reason with him to ease his cold heart,

"Mighty late this evening massa."

Beauford replied,

"What kinda ridin you plans on doin…gotta big day tomorrow suh."

Daniel looked at his friends with an evil smirk on his face and decided to impress them by displaying his authority,

"You do as ya told boy! Else I beat the skin right off of ya bones!"

Beauford looked at the three of them and took a deep breath. He looked up at the stars then down at

Annabelle. At that moment he was convinced that Daniel had an evil idea; so without causing any confusion, he gave Annabelle a kiss on the cheek and took her inside the cabin.

As Beauford walked into the room, he noticed Gladdia laying in bed sound asleep. He took slow, quiet steps toward the cradle to make sure that she was not awakened. Beauford positioned Annabelle in the cradle and said a prayer over her, asking God to protect and watch over her. Before walking outside, he walked over to Gladdia, kissed her on the cheek, and left out the front door. Once Beauford was outside on the porch, Daniel's friends walked forward and grab him by the arms. They position him on the horse with Daniel and tied his hands together. Afterwards, the four of them rode off into the dark fields, holding Beauford captive the entire night.

Early the next morning, Gladdia was awakened to the screeching sounds of Annabelle crying. As she looked over to Beaufords' side of the bed, she realized that he wasn't there. Assuming that he was out in the fields working, she arose from the bed, walked over to the cradle and grabbed Annabelle to calm her crying. Afterwards Gladdia took some spring water from an old bucket and began to give her and Annabelle a sponge bath. While doing this, she began to think on the argument her and Beauford had on the night before and became sadden. Not only was she upset about the argument, it disappointed her deeply that she could not give him a proper apology. So without any more delays, she swiftly prepared Annabelle and herself for work. Her plans were to leave early in hopes of running into Beauford in the fields.

After an half hour of preparing, Gladdia and Annabelle were dressed and ready for work. As Gladdia walked out the cabin door and down the porch steps; she positioned Annabelle in her arms comfortably and began walking through the Quarters. As Gladdia walked toward the fields, she began to notice Slaves running past her coming from every direction. She instantly became concerned and worried. Gladdia tried stopping a few of them to find out there reasons for running so frantically, but no one would answer. Finally out of no where, Big Debra ran up to her, she was short of breath and her eyes were full of tears,

"GLADDIE...GLADDIE...YA HAS TO COME SEE GLADDIE! SOMETHING BAD DONE HAPPENED...COME GLADDIE! HURRY!"

cried Big Debra as she locked arms with Gladdia and dragged her along to follow the others. As Gladdia ran through the fields with Big Debra, she could not help but worry for her husband. Where was he? Why wasn't he looking for her? As her and Big Debra got closer to the commotion she observed a body hanging from an oak tree. Although she could not recognize who it was, she felt herself becoming sad. It hurted her to see Slaves die that way on the Plantation.

Gladdia and Big Debra moved in closer to the scene to observe. Gladdia began to feel weak in the knees as she began to recognize the strange body hanging from the tree. They moved in closer to the scene. The closer they moved, the more upset Gladdia became. She stood there looking at the body in disbelief. The entire crowd that stood around became silent as she walked closer to the tree. She looked up at the body hanging there and recognized that it was her husband Beauford. Gladdia stood their holding her baby in disbelief. Suddenly she became hysterical, as she held Annabelle tightly in her arms. She fell down to her knees and began screaming and crying.

"LAWD!..OH LAWD NOOO!"

she cried out as Big Debra and the others surrounded her. Gladdia sat on her knees, arms folded and body trembling. She was crying and struggling to convince herself that she was having a bad dream, that maybe she would awaken to her husband laying beside her. As Big Debra walked over and took the baby away from her, she was convinced that she was not dreaming, but experiencing a tormenting encounter with the devil himself. As the others began to aid her in standing, she asked herself over and over; where is God? Why would he allow the devil to steal away someone that was so important to her and Annabelle?

She cried and cried; not for her loss, but for Annabelle's. She would never have an opportunity to experience life with both parents. On Williamsburg land, it was significant to have more than one guardian looking after you. Annabelle's days were expected to be harder from that day forward. The Slaves grieved in their hearts and gathered around Gladdia. They began walking with her to provide comfort in her time of sorrow. McAuthor and Daniel arrived at the scene minutes later. A look of disbelief appeared on both of their faces as they viewed the dead body of Beauford Perkins hanging from the oak tree; McAuthor shedded a silent tear in his honor.

Later on the next day, every Slave from the Plantation, including McAuthor and Jimmy gathered at the burial site alongside the church. They were all dressed in black to show respect and honor of Beauford's memorial service. Gladdia stood in front of the casket away from the others, embracing Annabelle in her arms and looking toward the sky. She appeared to be holding her emotions together effectively, yet there was something strange about her as if she had no concerns or emotions anymore. Suddenly there was a beautiful sound that extended from the crowd; it was the strong voice of Big Debra singing an old gospel hymn, "His Eye's On The Sparrow."

As she gained everyone's attention with her resilient voice, an emotional sensation began to warm everyone's heart. Listening to Big Debra sing during times of hardship gave everyone a sense of hope and reassurance.Gladdia listened to Big Debra sing. She held her daughter tightly in her arms and began to think back on her life, and all of the things that she encountered while living on the Plantation. There were so many questions in her mind that were unanswered, so many things about her life that caused confusion with her spirituality.

It was her belief that God had his reasons for everything that happened in the world, good or bad; but why was this happening to her? As tears rolled down her cheek, and pain rested in her heart, Gladdia began to sing along with Big Debra; softly. As they sang together, with Big Debra's voice in command; a voice from heaven began to speak these words to Gladdia.

"Everything will be okay, trials come to make you stronger. The race is not given to the swift, nor to the strong; but to the one who endureth until the end".

At that moment, Gladdia knew it was the voice of her creator. She looked over at the casket; then at her beautiful daughter. She began to smile. It was apparent that her mother, who passed away years ago, was in heaven praying and interceding on her behalf. Even though Beauford's soul had departed from the Earth, Gladdia's mind was now at peace. She found comfort in knowing that God took time to speak to her during this hardship. He heard her voice in spite of everything. All was well in her soul. God proved himself to be faithful. Beauford's suffering was over.

IV

"Mama make him stop!....make him stop!"

cried Annabelle as Jamison chased her around the kitchen with a slimy frog in his hands. It was eight years since Beaufords' death. The older Annabelle became, the more Gladdia missed having him around. As the children continued to play with one another, she stood at the stove for a moment to reflect. Tears rolled down her cheek as she watched her daughter limp around the kitchen; too innocent to realize that she was crippled. In her blissful mind she was perfectly normal. Annabelle had a heart that was filled with so much life and happiness. It was no wonder why she and Jamison got along so well.

"Lawd I declare yall carry on like some wild animals round here, sho nuff!"

 yelled Gladdia as she held each one by the arm, standing them beside one another.

"Now yall git rid of dat thing else ya end up eatin it fo supper!"

she continued jokingly as she smacked Jamison on the rear end.

He grabbed Annabelle by the hand and they both ran from the kitchen. Shortly thereafter, Maryrose walked into the kitchen wearing her satin night gown and matching robe. She sat down at the kitchen table. Gladdia greeted her with a warm hello,

"Howdy doo ma'am…I's jus gettn supper started here."

"Very well Gladdie."

Maryrose replied,

"Very well…those two youngins sho makes a lot of racket round here!"

Gladdia listened and took a deep breath. She continued to stir the pot of soup that's simmered on the stove. She found it hard to imagine why Maryrose would complain of the noise from the children when she's hardly around to even be bothered with it, however; she smiled to herself and replied,

"Yes ma'am ….humph! reckon dey do!"

Maryrose heard Gladdia's reply, but did not respond. She stared at the back of Gladdia's head in disgust. Even though she tolerated her working in the home, she felt awkward about having her there, especially when Daniel is around. Maryrose reached toward the center of the table for her regular drinking glass and walked toward the refrigerator. She poured herself a glass of orange juice and made a suggestion,

"Think maybe its bout time dat gal of yours git to workin round here huh!"

Gladdia heard Maryrose's idea and felt her heart drop. She knew that eventually Maryrose would start complaining about Annabelle not working, but she never expected it to be this soon. Annabelle walked with a limp. This caused Gladdia to worry about releasing her into the fields. Her only hope was to convince Maryrose that the best place for her was in the house by her side, but how could she convince her of this concept. As sweat developed on her forehead from the steam of the boiling pot, she swallowed the lump in her throat and replied softly with her plea,

"She not be in the way round here is she? Pretty quiet round here til Jamison come home from school…..reckon dey jus be mighty glad to play wit one anotha….I tries to keep an eye on both of em' best way I knows how"

Maryrose closed the refrigerator door and returned back to the kitchen table to sit down and enjoy her drink while Gladdia stood at the stove. She thought about Gladdia's explanation and replied boastfully,

"Anna not be in the way round here….jus time for her to start doin her share like the rest of ya!....my papi used to always say: if they can talk…they can work"

Gladdia was overwhelmed by Maryrose's suggestion. She felt herself become more and more worried. She had no other choice but to put her little pride aside and beg her to allow Annabelle to remain in the house. So without any procrastination, she turned off the fire from the stove and walked over to the table where Maryrose was sitting to state her appeal,

"Miss Patterson, I's find something right chere in dis house fo her to do to keep busy…..on count she got a bad leg, wont do much good out dere in the fields, she jus git in the way and make a mess a thangs, I make sho she work real hard Miss Patterson….you'll see!"

Maryrose sat at the table and contemplated Gladdia's proposal. Even though she wanted to be cruel and send Annabelle to the fields, her main concern was to keep her vastly occupied and away from Daniel's arms. Thus having her daughter work in the home could help achieve this secretive scheme. Maryrose grabbed her glass of orange juice and walked toward the kitchen window. She slowly drawed the curtains apart and replied,

"I spose it will be alright for now!.....but the minute I find her round here doin nothin but runnin round corrupting my boy, that gal is OUT into the fields!....cant afford not one more lazy nigger!"

Gladdia was quiet for a moment. Even though she was happy that Maryrose considered her request, it made her feel ashamed and disgusted to hear her refer to Annabelle as a "lazy nigger." Instead of getting upset, she made a choice to count her blessings and thank God for giving her favor with Maryrose,

"Yes ma'am!"

Gladdia answered,
"I's make sho she works real hard ma'am."

Maryrose was shocked with Gladdia's response but impressed in a peculiar way. She felt a sense of dominance in this situation which convinced her of the power she had over her. Maryrose walked from the window toward the kitchen door,

"Wont be too much longer fo we be needin ya round here anyway."

Maryrose said,

"Soon my Jamison be ole enough to care for himself and you and dat gal can both return to the fields!"

As Maryrose prepared to leave the kitchen, she was encountered by Hattie and Jimmy,

"Howdy doo! Miss Patterson"

Jimmy said in a warm voice.

When Jimmy spoke, the sound of his voice had an unusual effect on Maryrose, causing a chill to run down her spine. She turned and looked at him strangely as if there was a sexual attraction to him. Even though Jimmy was a house Slave and Daniel's most loyal servant, she often wondered how it would be if the two of them were to experience a sexual affair; but could she bring herself to do something so evil? If there was any chance of satisfying her curiosity, she needed to be alone with him away from all distractions,

"Don't forget to clean out the storage areas in the back!"

Maryrose said to him in hopes that he would go there directly.

"Gits right to it ma'am."

Jimmy replied excitedly, as he turned and headed back out of the kitchen door. Maryrose followed behind, but instantly decided not to pursue her cunning idea, for fear of being caught in the act. Instead she poured herself a glass of red wine and strolled upstairs to her bedroom for a short nap. Meanwhile, McAuthor decided to spend a little time with Annabelle and Jamison down by the fig tree. He spent a lot of time with them weekly; reading bible stories and teaching them spiritual values. It was McAuthors' goal to move to Canada and become and ordained minister. He spent all of his free time practicing his lectures and sermons with the children.

Annabelle and Jamison enjoyed their time with McAuthor. It gave them an opportunity to learn more about God and less time in the house doing chores.

"Want you to always remember that God created us all."

He would tell them,

"We should always love one another as God loves us."

It was important to McAuthor that they understood Gods promises for them, and that he was against slavery and inequality. One evening, as the three of them sat under the fig tree enjoying their conversations, Jamison looked across the field and observed Daniel walking toward them. Quickly McAuthor noticed and gestured for the children to stand up from the ground, and wash up for dinner. McAuthor recognized that Daniel was against his teachings, and he did not want the children to witness any argueing or yelling. McAuthor greeted Daniel with a warm welcome as he arrived at the fig tree.

"Howdy their Daniel!.....how was your visit down at the Richmond Place?"

he asked as he brushed dirt from the back of his trousers.

"Business as usual."

Daniel replied,

"Gotta few Slaves he wants to trade off...may even sell him a few."

McAuthor pretended to be interested in the conversation, but deep inside he hated to partake in discussions that involved Slavery or separating black families. He listened carefully to Daniel, making sure to pay close attention to his ideas and strategies involving the Plantation.

"Been thinking bout selling Gladdies gal."

Daniel said calmly,

"She be old enough to work in the fields... thinking she may git in the way round here wit her bad leg and all."

As McAuthor stood there and listened to Daniels' suggestion, he became furious. It was no secret that he had a soft heart for the Slaves, however; Annabelle held a special place in his heart since the day she was born.

"That little girl is jus as able to work on this Plantation as anyone else and you know it!"

he yelled out angrily,

"She lossed her pa when she was jus a baby, all she has is her mother, where is your compassion Daniel!"

Daniel immediately became frustrated with McAuthor. It made him highly upset when he demonstrated respect for the Slaves on the

Plantation, especially when it involved a business proposition. He began to yell at McAuthor,

"Compassion!. Don't tell me about compassion. I am low on sugar- cane and crop because I allow my Slaves to eat from shares. I allow then to have church, burials, weddings, and celebrations here on my land!!!! So don't go telling me nothing bout compassion!.....cant understand why you care so much for em."

McAuthor walked closer to Daniel. He looked him straight in the eyes and replied with a low stern tone,

"I come with the love of God in my heart....that same love I have for mankind.....it is that same love that you secretly have for that little girls mother!"

McAuthor then turned and walked away from Daniel; leaving him to think more about his decision making regarding Gladdia and Annabelle.

Later on that evening, all the Slaves completed their work in the fields. Big Debra decided to pay a visit to her oldest son Jimmy. As she walked through the Slave Quarters, she noticed him throwing away things from the storage shed. She began to head toward his direction in hopes of having quality time before he returned to the main house.

As she walked into the storage shed, she found him straightening out shelves and rearranging boxes.

She stood in the doorway and called out to him in a soft motherly voice,

"Jimmy."

she said gently.

When he heard the sound of his moms' voice, he turned around from the shelves and ran over to hug her tightly.

"Mama! How are you mama?"

he asked with excitement.

Big Debra pulled away from him slowly and straightened her white apron which protected her dress from dirt stains.

"Be's holdin up jus fine I reckon."

She replied,

"had to come check on ya….see how my Jimmy be doin, ya aint been down to the Quarters to see us in a while, had to see how deys treatin ya up here."

Jimmy pulled up an old chair and sat down, as Big Debra stood over him. He wrapped his arms around her legs and rested his head there. He felt a sign of relief enter his body, the kind you feel when you're surrounded by a mother's love. He became vulnerable for a moment.

"Be's alright mama."

He replied in a low voice,

 "Jus get confused mama, feel like I should be more than what I am…thinkin maybe the good lawd meant for me to be more than jus a house Slave, like maybe I should do somethin important."

Afterward, he stood from the chair and gestured for Big Debra to have a seat. Big Debra sat down and they quickly changed the subject,

"So how are Noah and Eliza?"

 he asked.

"Dey all be jus fine."

Big Debra replied,

"I Has Vynna keep an eye on em while I sit here witcha."

As Big Debra sat there and continued talking, Jimmy held his head down in sadness. He felt bad about being away from his family for so long.

 "I wish I could see you all more."

he said.

Big Debra could sense his sincerity. She looked up at him, grabbed his hand and gave him a big smile,

"Don't'cha go worrying yoself bout us!"

she said proudly,

"We all be doin jus fine! Ya know....I named you afta ya great grand papi!... I member he would sit me down on his lap and he say, "chile, trouble ought not to last always."…..seem like when he say dat my heart would smile; and I knew dat the good lawd would take care of me….Jimmy ya has to member dat errythang we goes through here is apart of our journey to a better place one day….it makes us stronger Jimmy and wiser!"

Jimmy looked at his mother with tears in his eyes. He kneeled down in front of her and layed his head on her lap.

"Wish I could jus take us all away from here mama, be a betta man and make ya proud of me."

Big Debra looked at Jimmy and felt so much joy in her heart. As tears filled her eyes from all the emotion, she took her hand and lifted his head from her lap. While looking into his eyes, she said to him tenderly,

"I's be right proud of ya nah son!"

Those words instantly brought a spirit of exhilaration into there space. As the two of them smiled and allowed themselves to be overwhelmed by the ambiance; Daniel walked in and caused a disturbance by his very own existence.

"If ya wanna have a moment wit yo mama, best do it on ya own time BOY!"

 He rudely announced as he looked down at them with disgust.
	Jimmy quickly stood from the ground and motioned for Big Debra to leave.

 "Yes suh massa!"

Jimmy replied,

	"Mama was jus leavin here suh."
	Big Debra took a look at Jimmy for one last time; then began to head toward the doorway. As Big Debra left the storage shed, Daniel suggested that Jimmy continued with his cleaning duties in a timely manner, and left him alone. Once Jimmy stood there alone in the shed, a feeling of depression over powered his heart. Even though it was set in his mind to accept his life as a Slave, he still suffered from confusion and bewilderment. He walked over to the chair, slowly sat down and looked toward heaven to have a conversation with God.

"Lawd….hope ya can hear me!.....I's tide a livin dis way lawd!....aint no way for a man to live. I needs strength!...Strength to be a man…I be's a man lawd….I BE'S A MAN!"

Jimmy cried out to God as if he were standing right beside him, and after spending ten minutes venting and weeping, he pulled himself together and continued on with his chores. After careful consideration, he felt a sense of strength and hope, as if he could endure any obstacle that came his way from that point on. He spent twenty more minutes cleaning and singing to God; then afterward he returned back to the house to help with dinner.

After leaving Jimmy in the storage shed, Daniel walked into the dining area to join his family for dinner. Everyone seemed to be in a joyful mood. They all sat at the dining room table sharing conversation. A young male Slave stood over them waving large feather fans to cool them off as Gladdia, Ola and Hattie paced in and out of the room, delivering food items to the dinner table.

Daniel instantly became excited and eager to have dinner with them all.

"Well good Lord, was beginning to wonder if ya ever show up for dinner!"

Maryrose said as she sat at the table sipping on her lemonade,

"If ya waited any longer the food would have been cold."

Daniel looked at Maryrose with a smile on his face, unfolded his napkin and placed it across his lap; then replied,

"Had business affairs to tend to at the Richmond Plantation earlier today… was thinking bout maybe doing a trade or selling a few Slaves round here, however; your brother here seems to feel as though I should keep the Slaves close to their families".

McAuthor listened to Daniel speak about selling and trading Slaves. He did not want Gladdia and the others to hear the conversation and become worried. He politely asked them all to step into the kitchen. After the Slaves left the room, McAuthor began to express his feelings to Daniel concerning the subject,

"I told you already Daniel, I think it's a bad idea to sell Gladdie's lil girl, poor Gladdia has suffered enough with Beauford killing himself and all."

Daniel became upset with McAuthor and his suggestion and they began to argue, they spent over ten minutes yelling back and forth discussing the benefits and burdens of trade selling. They caused such a ruckus until Maryrose interrupted them,

"Alright!!...alright!!!"

 she said,

"I personally told Gladdia that she can keep little Annabelle here in the house, as long as she works hard and stays outta the way…..so THERE! Problem solved!...now can we PLEASE eat our dinner in peace!"

Daniel looked over at Maryrose and listened to her suggestion. Deep inside he recognized her devious reasons for allowing Annabelle to stay on the Plantation, however; due to the guilt that he felt inside for secretly sleeping with Gladdia, he decided to keep the peace by not argueing with her. They became so involved in their conversation until they forgot all about little Jamison sitting there absorbing every word.
He listened for a little while longer, then positioned his spoon down on the table. He looked up at Daniel with a puzzled look on his face,

"Hey pa!...why cant Annabelle have dinner with us?"

 he asked.

Daniel and Maryrose looked at each other confusingly and ignored Jamisons' question,

"Just eat your dinner son, no need to worry about little Annabelle."

Daniel replied as he rose from the table to pour a glass of wine.

McAuthor heard Jamison and was instantly pleased with the question he asked; he decided to use that opportunity to provoke Daniel by asking him a cynical question of his own,

"Well Daniel, aren't ya gonna explain to the boy why we can't allow Annabelle to eat at the dinner table wit us?"

Maryrose looked at the two of them, she was aware that the conversation could make a turn for the worst so she began praying silently. Daniel took a sip of wine then leaned against the bar. He looked over at McAuthor, then at his son. They were both sitting there awaiting his answer.

"Son, it wouldn't be proper to have a Slave eat at the dinner table wit us!"

he replied,

"Dey belong out back in the kitchen wit the other Slaves, just as we belong here together.....you see Slaves prefer to be with their own kind son, it's the way we all prefer it to be."

Jamison looked at his father with more confusion then recalled a conversation that him, Annabelle and McAuthor shared under a fig tree.

"But papa!. Uncle McAuthor says that we all should be together, and love one another as God loves us. Right uncle?"

McAuthor looked at Jamison and smiled, "That's' right boy."

Daniel was so disturbed by what he heard until he could hardly think straight. He poured himself another glass of wine and sipped on it slowly. Maryrose stood up and slammed her knife on the kitchen table,

"Pardon me please, Ive seen to have lossed my appetite!"

Maryrose left the dining area while the others continued to eat their dinner. Daniel decided to have a private conversation with McAuthor. He summoned for Gladdia to remove Jamison from the dinner table. As Gladdia helped Jamison into the kitchen with his food, McAuthor began to rise from the table and speak out,

"Its gettin rather late Daniel, think I will turn in for bed now."

Daniel walked toward the dinner table and replied,

"Sit down Author, this will only take a minute."

McAuthor had a good feeling of what Daniel wanted to discuss with him, so without any hesitation, he sat back down at the table to await the one on one discussion.

Daniel stood in front of the dinner table and sipped the last of his wine before speaking,

"I allow you to walk round here being self righteous and talk about your God and his love for all mankind, but forcing your beliefs on my boy is where I draw the line!"

McAuthor became upset with Daniel's comfrontation. He is serious about his beliefs and his relationship with God. His feelings over powered him for a moment, causing him to yell out to Daniel,

"ALLOW! YOU DON'T ALLOW ANYTHING DANIEL, I AM A MAN! AND INCASE YOU HAVE FORGOTTEN, THIS HERE PLANTATION WAS LEFT TO ME AND MY SISTER!!!!!...MAYBE IT'S TIME YOU REMEMBER WHOSE LAND YOUR FEET STAND ON!"

Daniel walked away from the table. McAuthor caused him to feel guilty and embarrassed of his actions. As he walked toward the bar to prepare another glass of wine he spoke out to McAuthor in a low serious tone,

"If you wanna be a nigger lover dats your problem, but you will not destroy my boys way of thinking....he will be overseer of the Slaves one day, he needs to understand how the way of the world works! I wont have you confuse him with your fancy quotes from the bible."

McAuthor rose from the table, walked toward Daniel and looked him in the eye,

"You know it's not your son who is confused!"

 he said,

"Maybe you should take a look in the mirror….that little slave girl who is running around here playin with your son could have very well been a result of YOU being a negro lover……or have you forgotten."

Daniel slammed his wine glass on the bar and cried out loudly,

 "She is NOT my daughter!"

McAuthor looked at Daniel and took a deep breath; then walked away from him toward the dining room exit. Before leaving the room, he turned around to look at Daniel one last time,

"Well I pray for her sake that she's NOT!"

he replied.

Daniel held his head down in shame after hearing the remark. McAuthor left Daniel in the

dining area to ponder his thoughts and actions
regarding Jamison and his nurturing.

Gladdia finished her work in the Plantation
house and decided to head back to her cabin with
Annabelle. As the two of them reached the front
porch and walked into the dark area of the cabin,
Gladdia burned a lantern to provide light and
positioned Annabelle into her bed. As she tucked
her in tightly and gave her a kiss on the cheek, she
turned around and discovered Daniel standing in
the corner of the room.
Gladdia screamed out in terror, and tried to run
away from him. He grabbed her and threw her
across the room into the bed. Annabelle had never
experienced this type of disruption with her
mother. She sat up in her bed and cried out to her
mom. As Gladdia tussled with Daniel on the bed,
fighting to keep him from violating her, she
couldn't help but focus more on her daughter who
sat there watching her get sexually abused.
Gladdia managed to rise from the bed. She
immediately ran toward Annabelle to comfort her;
almost instantly Daniel grabbed her by the neck
and threw her back unto the bed, this time
restraining her more with his body weight. She
was helpless. As Annabelle sat in her bed crying in
the background, Daniel slowly began kissing
Gladdia on her neck, not in an aggressive way, but

real passionately, as if she was his wife. He began to touch her body in ways that only Beauford would. Daniel whispered words in her ear like, "this feels so good" and "I've been thinking about you all day."

As Daniel put himself inside of Gladdia, she began to experience something that she had never experienced with him before. He had become more intimate and affectionate with her, causing the encounter to be more likeable and somewhat enjoyable. In times past, Gladdia would close her eyes and pray to God, asking him to help relieve her of the pain and hurt she would feel in her heart, yet this time she tried something different. While Daniel was inside of her thrusting slowly and passionately, she closed her eyes and pretended that she was with her Beauford and that everything was perfect.

Daniel began to kiss on her more aggressively, making his way down to her cleavage area. Gladdia became overwhelmed with emotion and began to breathe and moan uncontrollably. The more she imagined herself being with Beauford, the more excited her body became and as Daniel started thrusting harder inside of her, Annabelle's cry in the background began to slowly fade away. The two of them made love to one another until they reached a level of culmination, causing them both to yell out in great euphoria.

As their moment of pleasure ended, Daniel lied on Gladdia for a moment. He was breathing hard on her neck and rubbing his hands through her hair. She opened her eyes and looked over his shoulders at her daughter sleeping across the room. She couldn't help but wonder to herself if what she did was wrong in the eyes of God.

Although Daniel had been forcing himself on her for years, she had never enjoyed any encounters with him until that moment. Did this make her a bad person? Was she wrong for pretending that he was her husband? As tears slowly dropped from her eyes, Daniel arose from the bed and left without saying a mumbling word. Gladdia lied still in the bed for hours. She stared at the ceiling until she fell asleep.

After leaving the Slave Quarters, Daniel walked into the house sneakily. He slowly walked up the staircase and down the hall. He took a peep into his son's bedroom to make sure he was sound asleep. He continued down the hall until he reached his bedroom. When he walked in, he found Maryrose still awake, looking out of the window. She turned to face him and said softly,

"Had me worried....it's the third time this week you've been late to bed."

Daniel paused for a moment, then took off his shirt and crawled into bed facing the opposite direction. He pulled the thin blanket over his sholders,

"Had to check on a few things in the Quarters."

he replied

.

Maryrose walked closer to the bed and looked down at Daniel,

"DANIEL!"

she cried out with tremble in her voice,

"I am your wife and I deserve to know what's goin on right this instant!....what kinda example are you being for our SON!"

Daniel just lied in bed and continued to face the opposite direction. He took a deep breath and responded in a nonchalant manner,

"Got an early morning Mary...best git in bed and git some sleep."

Maryrose didnt say anything else. She understood that Daniel did not care about her feelings and was not willing to compromise. She walked closer to the bed, crawled in slowly and faced the opposite direction; her back turned to him. As she lay there with tears in her eyes she began to wish that her mother was still alive. It was her knowledge and wisdom that would help her get through these hard times. She went through the same issues with her husband. Big Debra was his bed Slave for years before he passed away. Why was Beauford so obsessed with sleeping with Gladdia? Why would he put their marriage in harms way? Maryrose had no solutions or answers. Her and Gladdia were being forced to cry themselves to sleep in the same night over the same man; dealing with the same hurt.

Early the next morning, Gladdia and Annabelle were walking through the Slave Quarters as usual, headed toward the Plantation house for work. As they walked with each other side by side, watching the other field Slaves pass them by. Gladdia stopped and looked Annabelle in her eyes,

"Time ya knew!"

she said,

"Wonts be able to run round wit Jamison no mo, ya be's old enuff to work nah…..gone be workin right lone wit me in the kitchen…..massa not wontcha laggin round."

Annabelle began to look sad. She could not understand why she wasn't able to play with Jamison anymore. Even though there were other Slaves on the Plantation who were her age, she was the closest with Jamison and enjoyed playing around with him.

Once they arrived to the Plantation house, they immediately began working. The first thing they started on while Maryrose prepared Jamison for school was scrubbing the dining room floor. As they were on there knees cleaning, Annabelle was reminded of what McAuthor told her and Jamison about loving one another and found herself becoming confused, she looked over at Gladdia and asked,

"Mama! Why me and Jamison not be able to be round each otha no mo….massa or Miss Patterson not like me?"

Gladdia felt bad about the question Annabelle asked her, she didnt want her to be worried about Maryrose and Daniels hatred. Although the Patterson's were not too fund of Annabelle, or any other Slave for that matter, Gladdia did not inform Annabelle of that. She took another approach instead,

"Now dontcha go thinking that way chile."

she answered,

"Jus the ways of the world dats all….white folk don't like their Slaves gettn to close to em, deys be afraid we jus might learn something valuable."

Gladdia giggled to herself and continued scrubbing the floor, Annabelle responded in a confused manner,

"Well mama, massa McAuthor say we spose to always love one anotha, no matta what dey looks like or who dey are."

Gladdia immediately became frustrated, and slammed the deck brush on the floor,

"Well dat po white man aint gon rest til massa Patterson has him swingin round here from a tree wit the rest of dem loose lip Slaves."

She took her hand and lifted Annabelle's chin so that there eyes were looking at one another,

 "Chile, ya must neva let the massa hear ya talk dat way, don't matta if it be right or wrong; be betta to jus stay quiet bout the whole thang. Ya gots to learn to stay alive round here chile, an talkn bout Slaves an white people lovin each otha not be a good way."
      Annabelle didnt say anything, she just nodded her head in agreement and they both continued to scrub the floor.

      Later on that evening, Daniel and Maryrose decided to invite a few friends over from the Richmond Plantation for dinner and socializing. All servants were present and dressed in their formal uniforms. The dining room table was set to perfection with expensive china and fine linen. Ola and Hattie silently stood in the rear awaiting instructions, while Gladdia and Annabelle brang food items out from the kitchen.
      Elnora and Jackson Richmond were the guest of honor for the evening, they were the owners of the Richmond Plantation where Daniel conducted a lot of his business concerning Slave trade and auctioning. As they sat at the table enjoying conversation, Gladdia and Annabelle delivered the last of the food items.

"Dinner smells lovely!"

announced Daniel as he watched Gladdia position the stuffing on the table,

"Yea, smells great girls."

McAuthor reiterated.

"Why thankya massa, we do our best round here wit the lawd help."

replied Gladdia as her and Annabelle placed the bread and butter on the dinner table.

As Annabelle positioned everything properly on the table, she accidentally dropped a bowl of green beans on the floor. Ola and Hattie, who were standing in the rear rushed over to help her. Jamison quickly jumped down and began to aid Annabelle in cleaning. Gladdia politely moved him out of the way and replied,

"Mighty kind of ya massa Jamison, but we's take care of it."

As she guided him back to his seat and continued to help out with the cleaning, Daniel became embarrassed because of his sons actions and his willingness to help. He did not want his guests to believe that he was raising his son to love Negroes. He looked over at Jackson and made an attempt to clear up the confusion with a derisive comment,

"Seems that my son doesn't know the difference tween a horse and an ass!"

Daniel said as he took a sip from his glass of apple cider. Jackson looked at his wife Elnora, then back at Daniel and smiled,

"Dats why it is important to train ya kids on proper Plantation value."

Jackson replied,

"Once he's older…..you should consider sending him to my camp at Richmond!....He can be trained on proper Slave mastering. I will offer you a reasonable price and insure that the boy learns everything!!!"

As Jackson made his gesture at the dinner table, Ola and Hattie finished with the cleaning and returned to the rear of the room. Gladdia hauled Annabelle off to the kitchen. Jamison stared at her from the dinner table as she left the room. Jackson noticed Annabelle's limp but did not say anything.

Jackson continued to speak about the benefits of the camp at Richmond Plantation.the more he spoke on the issue, the more frustrated McAuthor became; yet he was able to maintain himself and remain a gentleman.

As time moved forward and everyone completed their dinner course, Gladdia and

Annabelle returned to the dining area to help clear the table, once again; Jackson noticed Annabelle's limp in her walk, yet this time; he made a decision to ask Daniel about it,

"She hurt her leg?"

Jackson asked as he handed over his dishes to Gladdia.

"Not at all."

Daniel replied,

"She was born that way, figured she be more useful in the kitchen than in the fields so we keeps her in to help with chores and cookin."

Jackson took a sip of cider from his glass and replied,

"I commend you on your kindness…a crippled Slave would never survive on my Plantation. Cant afford to have one takin up space, best to end their lives when they're born……save you the headache later."

Maryrose and Elnora witnessed the conversation but made no comments. It is Southern tradition for a lady to allow her husband to do most of the talking at the dinner table while in the midst of company. After hearing the comments made by Jackson, everyone; especially Jamison, became upset and irritated. Even though Daniel and Maryrose had the tendency to be cold hearted people, they did not believe in killing Slaves. They believed in raising them to be strong hard workers in the Plantation house and in the fields.

McAuthor looked over at Jamison; sitting there looking sad with his head held down. He decided to take him away from all of the talk concerning killing crippled Slaves.

"C'mon soldier!"

McAuthor replied excitedly,

"How bout we get you washed up and ready for bed…..maybe even tell you a bedtime story….c'mon now!"

Jamison held his head up and gave McAuthor the biggest smile ever. He enjoyed spending time with his uncle and the thought of hearing a bedtime story made him extremely thrilled to leave the dinner table. As they prepared to leave the dining area, Maryrose and Elnora decided to sit out on the front porch for a glass of Brandy while Jackson and Daniel enjoyed a cigar in the living room. The four of them spent the remainder of the evening socializing with one another and discussing topics that they wouldn't dare mention at the dinner table. Meanwhile; Gladdia, Annabelle, along with Ola and Hattie were in the kitchen washing dishes, cleaning the floor, and putting things away for the night.

As the evening grew late, Maryrose and Daniel prepared themselves to say goodnight to their guests

"Goodbye now! And thank you so much for having dinner wit us!"

yelled Maryrose as her and Daniel stood out on the porch waving to Jackson and Elnora. Due to Daniels' traveling and Jackson's camp meetings, it was hard for the four of them to spend any time together. Thus saying goodbye was a cheerless occasion. Nevertheless, they were thankful for the moments shared together and looked forward to many more. As the Richmond's rode away, Maryrose turned and walked through the front door of their home. She decided to pour herself one last drink of wine before heading to bed.

"Gonna go upstairs to bed."

she said softly to Daniel while pouring,

"Will you be joining me darling?"

Daniel sat down on the sofa to light his pipe. His deceitful ways had influenced him to make other plans but he did not allow Maryrose to figure them out. He inhaled smoke from his pipe and replied

"I will be there shortly my dear, go ahead and wait for me there."

Maryrose looked over at Gladdia as she walked to and fro. She began to feel an evil rage for her, as if she were an enemy. Even though Daniel had not yet openly admitted to sleeping with Gladdia, Maryrose was aware that she was the reason for his disappearing acts; which occured regularly. She swallowed her pride and replied annoyingly,

"Very well then! I will see you upstairs shortly."

As Maryrose left the dining area, Gladdia returned to the room to finish clearing the dinner table. Daniel sat on the sofa, smoking his pipe and thinking sexual thoughts about Gladdia. The alcohol in his system caused him to feel a certain urge that he could hardly contain.

"Have Hattie and the others finish in here."

Daniel said to her calmly,

"Wish to see you in the storage shed out back, wait for me there."

Gladdia took a deep breath and positioned a bowl on the dinner table. Deep inside she had a strange feeling that Daniel wanted to be sexually pleasured by her, which caused her heart to beat steadily and develop feelings of anxiety. She knew that she had no other choice in the matter. She had to obey his commands. She replied graciously,

"Yessuh, right away suh!"

As Gladdia walked through the kitchen headed to the storage shed, Daniel walked over to the bar to pour one more glass of wine. Even though he enjoyed having sexual intercourse with Gladdia, being intoxicated helped him to deal with the guilty feelings that flooded his heart due to infidelity.

Thirty minutes passed away and Daniel found himself highly intoxicated. It was that moment when he decided to make his way to the storage shed to see Gladdia. He took one last sip of his wine and walked through the kitchen. As he headed to the back door; Hattie, Ola, and Annabelle look at him strangely. Even though they showed no signs, they were aware of the situation, and could hardly hide their feelings of anger.

As Daniel walked out the back door toward the storage shed, he heard Gladdia's voice in the wind, humming a gospel hymn. As he got closer to the shed and peeped in through the front door, he saw her pacing the floor. Before she noticed him, he walked in slowly behind and grabbed her from the back. He frightened her,

"Oh massa! Ya like to scare me half to death"

she said worriedly.

Daniel grabbed her by the arms and turned her around to face him. He began kissing her on the neck and attempted to untie her dress. Gladdia struggled to break free,

"Massa pleeeeease!.....dont do it suh!....dont do it!"

she cried out woefully.

Daniel slapped her in the face so hard until she fell to the ground. He looked down at her laying there helpless and in despair. The fact that she was powerless and had no control caused him to desire her more. As he unbuttoned his shirt and unzipped his trousers, he spoke to her in a low tone,

"You belong to me and you will do as you are told!"

Daniel then dropped down on the ground. He lied on top of her and kissed her passionately on the neck. He did not remove her dress, he reached between her legs and ripped away her bloomers. As he placed himself inside of Gladdia, tears began to fall slowly from her eyes, how could she ever bring herself to endure this cruelty? Daniel kissed her on the neck harder, then down to her breast cavity. He thrusts himself harder inside of her until she began to make loud noises from the pain.

"I love you Gladdie!.....I love you!"

He said softly in her ear as he thrusts harder and harder, Gladdia did not respond, instead she said a prayer to herself hoping that it would all end quickly. Then suddenly she remembered what she did before when Daniel forced himself upon her down in the Quarters. She closed her eyes and imagined that Daniel was her husband Beauford, only this time she became more accustomed. Gladdia began to enjoy Daniel pleasuring her; she even started responding back to him by making comments like, "I love you" and "This feels so good."

The more she imagined Daniel being her husband, the easier it became to tolerate him and before long it was almost over. As both of them reached their climax, Daniel rested on top of Gladdia, breathing hard on her neck for seconds. The moment she opened her eyes and realized what had transpired between the both of them, she began to feel worst than before and tears flooded her eyes.

Minutes later Daniel arose from the ground, quickly put on his clothes and left her laying there in the storage shed. When he departed he did not notice McAuthor hiding on the side of the storage shed. McAuthor witnessed the entire occurrence between the both of them and was very displeased with Daniels' disposition. As he sat there battling his feelings of confusion, he could only ask himself the questions: How long does Daniel intend to keep secretly sleeping with Gladdia? And why does it seem as if she was enjoying it?

V

It was spring of 1846. Everyone in the Quarters, including Jamison and Jimmy were leaving from church service; talking and laughing with one other. As everyone gathered in the church yard to plan their evenings with one another, Gladdia walked beside Big Debra and listened while she updated her on the latest gossip in the Quarters. Suddenly Jamison ran over to Annabelle while she was speaking with Eliza and grabbed her by the hand

"Hey Anna!...come I wanna show you somethin.."

Jamison quickly pulled Annabelle away from Eliza and they ran off together. Because of her leg disability, she had a hard time keeping up with him, as a result; he made a strong effort to hold on to her hand tightly to ensure that she didnt fall. Everyone waved goodbye to them as they departed.

As Gladdia watched her daughter limp along with Jamison into the distance, she turned to face Big Debra, who was standing beside her with her hands resting on her wide hips,

"Never seen nothin like it befoe."

she said,

"It's like dey one in the same, dey not see what us and the massa see....I's fraid for em Debra."

Big Debra grabbed Gladdia by the hand and looked her deep in the eyes,

"Deys be jus fine Gladdie, they both older nah and the good lawd be watchin over em'.....ya cant keep two people apart who loves each otha no matta how hard ya try!......deys spirit be's the same, its gone last a long time and one day set em free from all dis!....you see...Now come on yall!"

As Big Debra gestures for everyone to follow her, they all left the church yard and headed back toward the Quarters for a big Sunday Feast with one another.

Meanwhile Jamison and Annabelle continued to run through the Plantation yard until they reached the plantation house. Once they arrived there, they creeped around to the back kitchen window where they found two cherry pies cooling. They both looked at one another with excitement, the aroma from the pies caused there mouths to water. Annabelle was a tad bit more excited than Jamison, she had never eaten cherry pie before; only apple.

"Sure smell awful good don't it?"

Jamison asked Annabelle as he licked his lips and rubbed his stomach.

"Yea!..I's reckon it do!"

replied Annabelle,

"Ya mama made those dint she?"

Jamison looked around to make sure no one was watching, then replied,

"Yeah, mama cooks em' every Sunday round dis time ya know…she sits em' here to cool off."

Annabelle held her head down, then lifted it slowly. She took one last peek at the scrumptious looking pies in the window,

"Ya know, I always wonder what a pie like dat would taste like,…it sho' looks good."
    Jamison looked at Annabelle cunningly, then took one more look around to make sure that no one was watching. He quickly took one of the pies from the window,

"Well why don't we jus FIND OUT!"

he yelled, then ran as fast he could with the pie in his hands, leaving Annabelle standing there with an alarmed look on her face,

"NOT SO FAST JAMISON!"

she yelled,

"WAIT FO' ME!"

Annabelle ran on her crippled leg behind Jamison as fast as she could. They both ran through the opened fields together laughing and breathing hard. They ran past the sugarcane fields, the pond, then finally they reached the fig tree. They sat down with their cherry pie to rest a bit. Jamison positioned the pie securely in his lap, making sure that it did not fall into the dirt,

"So ya never had cherry pie before Anna?"

he asked as he sat under the fig tree enjoying the aroma.

"May have."

Annabelle replied,

"But I's not member it lookin all pretty and smellin all good like dis one here; makes me wanna have a piece!"

Jamison and Annabelle both stared at the pie, then at one other. The warmth from the pie began to aggravate Jamison's legs, causing him to position it on the ground in between two stumps. They giggled from excitement.

"Well what ya waitin foe gal!"

Jamison asked hastily,

"Go head and git yaself a big ole piece!"

Annabelle looked at the pie and moved in closer. Deep inside she wanted to place her entire hand in the middle of that pie and eat it all at once, but she felt hesitant and somewhat awkward,

"Not sure I know how I spose to eat it."

she said softly.

Jamison began to feel embarrassed for her. He understood that because she is a Slave on the Plantation; she was only allowed to eat certain things, moreover; cherry pie from the kitchen was not one of those options. He leaned over and used his fingers to carefully pierce the edges of the pie for easy access. He began to demonstrate to her.

"Well ya jus grab a piece a pie like dis'…..and ya put it in ya
 mouth….like DIS'!"

Just before Jamison put the piece of pie to his lips, the high temperature from it caused his

fingers to burn and he dropped it on the ground;
they both laughed.

Here!...lemme try!"

Annabelle said excitedly as she reached for a
piece. She carefully grabbed a piece of pie and
leaned over to feed it to him. They look each other
in the eyes as she placed her fingers near
Jamisons' mouth. He grabbed the pie with his teeth
and lips. He gently grazed her fingers with his
warm wet tongue. Instantly a warm and tingly
sensation entered both of their bodies. They began
to look at each other differently in that second; not
as two young teenagers running around in the
fields, but as two people who were inadvertently
falling in-love with each other. Nonetheless, they
ignored those feelings and continued on with their
conversation.

"Reckon ya mama let me stay over for supper wit
yall tonite?"

Jamison asked, hoping that she would coincide
with the suggestion.

"Don't think she mind."

Annabelle answered,

 "But what for?....Aint ya mama fixin a good
supper for you and ya papi?"

Jamison was reminded of the relationship between his mother and father and became sad,

"Yea! Sunday be's the only day mama cook for us."

he replied,

"And today she made my favorite: chicken and biscuits, but her and pa yell at each other so much til I don't care much to be round it.....I....well I think my pa not like my mama too much."

Annabelle began to feel sorry for Jamison, she quickly made a suggestion in hopes that it would cheer him up,

"Spose we could ask mama together!"

she said excitedly,

"Will that make ya feel betta?"

Jamison stood up from the ground and reached for Annabelle's hand. She gave him her left hand while holding the pie in the other.

" I feels betta already!"

he said to her while wiping the dust from his trousers. Annabelle just smiled back at Jamison and replied,

"Well I guess we betta git goin then, I spec mama be cookin supper right about now, so we best go head and git it over with."

Jamison and Annabelle held hands and walked toward the Slave Quarters, they laughed with one another and enjoyed their pie. Once they finally reached Annabelle's cabin, the two of them walked in. They found Gladdia placing food on an old table. Neither one of them mumbled a single word. They stood next to one another in silence, waiting on the perfect opportunity to ask the big question. Even though Gladdia's back was turned to them, she sense their presence in the room,

"See's the two of ya standin dere!

she said in a sweet tone,

"Jamison, ya best be headed home fo ya papi come down here lookin fo ya…I spec he not seen ya all day."

Annabelle and Jamison looked at each other nervously. Even though both of them were hesitant, Annabelle could feel herself building enough courage. Without hesitation, she blurted out the question,

"Mama!... Jamison and I wanna know if it be okay for him to stay over wit us fo supper."

Gladdia heard Annabelle's question but did not respond immediately. She continued to place food on the table and ponder on the question that was asked.

"Only a little food."

she answered,

"Barely enough to feed I selves chile, nah massa Jamison must eat wit his own family."

Jamison became upset. Although he spent the majority of the day with Annabelle, he did not want to return home and be forced to listen to his mother and father argue with each other like children. He felt compelled to beg Gladdia, "Uhm Gladdie, I don't really eat a whole bunch, only a little will do me jus fine, I jus wanna have supper wit Anna, dats all!....I's go home right after! I promise!"

Gladdia saw the look in their eyes and realized how much they cared for one another, so in spite of how Daniel may have felt about it; she chose to allow him to stay.

"Well I spose ya need somethin in ya belly!"

she said,

"Afta all dat runnin around in the fields, wouldn't be decent to not feed ya when ya hungry, so I spose it be alright dis time!"

Gladdia smiled and put an extra bowl of stew on the table. She made a gesture for him to join in,

"Go head! Sit down right here...me and Anna will walk-ya home right afta!"

Everyone sat down at the table for dinner; Gladdia recommended that Annabelle and Jamison grab each others' hand while she said the blessing.

As she finished and they began eating their food, Gladdia looked across the table at them for five minutes. Her eyes filled with tears. Annabelle noticed her mother crying and became upset,

"mama! Why are ya cryin"

she asked,

Gladdia looked at the both of them; then used her apron to wipe away the tears from her eyes. She no longer had an appetite so she rose from the table and began speaking and pacing the floor.

"I always wondered what it would be like to sit at the dinner table with you, me and your papi. You were just a baby when he left us.....oh how I wish he were here right now."
Jamsion held his head down and continued to eat his food, Annabelle layed her spoon down on the table and looked up at Gladdia,

"So how did he die mama?....how did my papi die?"

Gladdia looked at her daughter with confusion, she wanted to tell her the cause of her fathers' death but she was having a hard time trying to explain. She did not feel that Annabelle was old enough to understand but she was aware that she had to give her an answer.
She walked over to Annabelle while she was eating and began telling the story.

"I wanted to wait til you were old enough to understand. Ya papi, he was a very good man, a warm, kind, strong, and hard working man. He was so proud of you when you were born. He made so many promises to the both of us and I believed him....oh how I believed him. When massa made me work in the kitchen, I had to bring you along wit me. Ya papi, he spent a lot of time alone, and the more time he spent alone, the more sad he became.....got to the point where it wasn't nothin I could do for em' anymore. Ya papi allowed the ways of dis Plantation to make him give up on his life…. So one night after we done fussin at each otha, ya papi left for a walk………it was the laz time I ever saw him alive, or even heard his voice….. I woke up the next day an we found em' hanging from an oak tree…ya papi took his own life chile."

Gladdia began crying softly; she left the room and walked outside for a minute to clear her mind.

Annabelle held her head down in shame. She began to cry for her mothers' pain. Jamison reached over across the table and held her hand to show a sign of comfort.

Later that evening after everyone was done eating, Gladdia and Annabelle made it their responsibility to walk Jamison home. They walked through the fields, laughing and enjoying small conversation. Once they arrived at the house, and walked up the steps of the porch, they noticed that the front door was opened and all lights were on. This situation was peculiar, for Jimmy was typically ordered to keep all doors closed and lights off at nightfall.

They slowly walked into the front living area. They found Maryrose passed out on the floor from intoxication. Jamison immediately became worried as Gladdia and Annabelle rushed over and made several attempts to lift her. Gladdia cried out,

"Oh lawd! Miss Patterson! You be's alright?....JIMMY!.....JIMMY BOY!....COME QUICK!!

Jimmy ran into the room and tried to help Gladdia while Annabelle and Jamison stood to the side holding each others hand. As they lifted Maryrose from the floor, she regained consciousness and began speaking to them rudely.

"What are ya doin!....where are ya takin me!....leave me alone.....LEAVE ME ALONE!"

Gladdia and Jimmy ignored Maryrose's rude behavior. They continued to work persistently at getting her up the staircase and into her bedroom. As they dragged her into the room and positioned her into bed, she continued to speak to them rudely. She geared her words more toward Gladdia,

"Ya ruined everything!......EVERYTHING!....I hate you!....you hear me nigger!....I HATE YOU!"

Suddenly Jimmy thought about Jamison, and how worried he must have been. He left Gladdia in the room and went to check on him. When he arrived to Jamison's bedroom, he was in bed safely with Annabelle standing beside him. Gladdia managed to get Maryrose undressed. She gave her a sponge bath, and tucked her in bed securely. Shortly thereafter she was sound asleep.Gladdia and Annabelle left and headed back to the Quarters later that night. Jimmy secured the house and went to sleep.

As Gladdia and Annabelle were holding hands and walking through the Quarters, they noticed Daniel from a distance. He was sitting on their porch and smoking on his pipe. Although it seemed rather strange, Gladdia knew exactly what he wanted. They stopped walking for a moment and stared at him. Gladdia could see the weird expression on his face. She was aware of what was about to transpire between the two of them.

"Anna, wont you to go down to Big Debra's til I come and git ya."

Gladdia said firmly as she grabbed Annabelle by the hand. She knew that Daniel was about to rape her again. She did not want her daughter to witness this horrible act of cruelty anymore. Annabelle ignored Gladdia's command. She considered all of the bad things that Daniel was capable of doing to her mother. She did not want to leave her alone with him. She began to cry softly.

"Mama …I's not leave ya, I stays right here wit ya!"

She replied as she stood next to her mother trembling with fear.

Annabelle's courage caused Gladdia to be proud. It produced a warm feeling inside. It did her heart good to know that her daughter possessed an act of courage, surely inherited from her father. Nevertheless; Gladdia insisted that she leave, for fear that Daniel may do something to harm her. Gladdia shouted out to Annabelle loudly,

"YOU DO WHAT I TELLYA NAH CHILE!"

 and without further wavering, Annabelle ran as fast as she could toward Big Debra's cabin.

Gladdia stood with her feet firmly to the ground. The nervousness of it all caused her to feel un-stable. She could barely hold her composure. She looked over at Daniel. A small voice inside was telling her to run away quickly, but she did not want to make Daniel angry. It seemed to be over quickly when she cooperated with him. She just walked toward him slowly. Her hands began to sweat. She wiped her palms on the edge of her torn dress as she moved in closer.

"Miss Patterson ....she be right sick. Ya may wanna go to the house to see bout her."

Gladdia made that comment in hopes that Daniel would re-direct his intentions and run off to see about his wife. But he just sat there with one thing on his mind, and he would not be satisfied until his urges were fulfilled. He looked at Gladdia with a lust hunger in his eyes,

"She not be the one who needs to be tended to right now."

Even though Gladdia swore to herself that she would not try to run, the thought of Daniel attacking her caused fright. She tried to run quickly passed him into the cabin but he caught her by the dress and ripped it
.
"Massa! Oh! Massa please!"

cried Gladdia, begging him to stop, but the begging only caused him to react more, as if he was stimulated from it. Daniel grabbed Gladdia by her arms and forced her into the cabin. As he hauled her into the bedroom, he whispered provocative words into her ear. The thought of it all caused her to feel sickly, and unworthy as a woman. She begged him to stop once again,

"Please massa, I beg you....pleeeease!"

Daniel ignored her plea and slapped her so severe until she fell prostrate across the bed. He looked down at her lying there helpless and vulnerable. Deep in her heart she felt that Daniel had nothing but hatred in his heart for her; otherwise, he wouldn't do such cruel things. Daniel did not hate Gladdia. He had been in-love with her for years, even before she was pregnant with Annabelle. He wasn't taught, nor did he ever think it was important to treat her with any respect. He was always taught by his father that Slaves enjoyed being treated harshly; that they weren't real humans with real emotions.

Daniel looked at Gladdia on the bed and ripped off his shirt aggressively, but before he fell down on top of her to engage in sexual interaction; McAuthor rushed into the room out of no where. He grabbed Daniel by the arms, turned him around to face him and commenced to hitting him in his face repeatedly. They fought in the cabin for several minutes, destroying everything in site. Gladdia sat in a corner crying and begging them to stop. After Daniel was worn out and beatened up from fighting, he broke away and ran swiftly towards the front door, but not without yelling the words:

"I'm gonna kill you for dis boy!"

McAuthor ran over to Gladdia whom was terrified, and hugged her tightly in his arms. He reassured her that this act would never happen again. She just hung her face in his chest and began to call on Jesus for strength. As she drenched his shirt with her tears, her only wish were to be dead. Gladdia never went for Annabelle that night, after McAuthor left; she decided to stay alone in the cabin and pray to God for peace of mind and strength.

Early the next day, Annabelle stood out in the Plantation yard hanging white linen on the clothes line to dry in the sun. Even though she still remained upset from the night before, Gladdia was in the kitchen showing no signs of worry or distress, neither one of them gave it much thought afterward. As she looked over across the yard, she observed Daniel and Maryrose standing on the porch; then Jimmy and Shadrach carried traveling bags to a wagon attached to a horse.

McAuthor walked out the front door of the house, also carrying two traveling bags. He put them into the wagon. He walked over to Jimmy and Shadrach, and gave them both a handshake. He walked over to Maryrose and gave her a big hug and kiss. It wasn't until that moment when Annabelle realized that McAuthor must have been leaving the Plantation for a while, but why?

McAuthor walked over to Jamison, who was standing aside with a sad look on his face. He attempted to give him a hug. Jamison opposed the gesture and broke out running into the fields. He ran passed Annabelle crying.

McAuthor looked out into the fields as Jamison ran off and noticed Annabelle hanging linen on the clothes line. He waved good-bye to her, she waved back. He then walked toward the wagon and climbed aboard. As the driver began to transport him away, Annabelle waved at him until he disappeared into the trees. She stood there for a minute. She never imagined what living on the Plantation would be like without him. McAuthor was a good man and a Godly man who loved everyone. She knew that she would miss him dearly. As a tear slowly ran down her cheek, she continued to hang linen on the clothes line and sing gospel hymns to herself.

After hanging all the linen, Annabelle was ordered by Maryrose to pick apples from the apple tree for homemade preserves. As she walked through the fields with her bucket filled with apples, she passed by Jamison sitting under the same fig tree that they always sit under; she joined him.

"Why ya reckon massa McAuthor left us?"

 she asked.

Jamison took an apple from the bucket and began taking small bites,

"Mama says he wants to go up North to Canada to become a minister."

He replied in a dreary tone. Annabelle looked at Jamison with a confused expression,

"Sounds like dat be far away, why he needs to go so far away to do dat?"

"Maybe it's cause everybody dere be free."

Jamison said as he continued to nibble on his apple,

"No slavery, or hate, uncle McAuthor always used to say he wanna live in a place where everyone be treated equally."

Annabelle heard something that she thought she would never hear. Could there really be a place in the world where everyone is free? Is there a place where slavery does not exist? She looked him straight in the eyes and asked him,

"Ya mean dere's a place where niggras like me are FREE?....no slavery?

Jamison rose up from the ground with his apple in his hand,

"Anna let me explain it all to ya…see in the North everyone is free and can do whatever dey please….even have real jobs and go to school. Uncle say not too many Slaves know bout it, on account the masters think dey may try to run off for dey freedom."

Annabelle took an apple from the bucket and began nibbling,

"Wonda why mama neva tells me bout it, she always say she wanna betta life fo' me."

"Well maybe you should tellya mama!"

Jamison replied,

"Maybe she not know bout it."

Annabelle thought about what Jamison had explained to her and became excited. She grabbed her bucket of apples,

"Think ima ask mama bout it…. figure if she don't know den maybe you can tell her what ya tol' me, and maybe one day we all can leave dis place!"

Annabelle was so excited until she walked swiftly toward the Plantation house. Although her leg caused her to walk slower than others, she learned how to adjust herself to walk at a faster pace. Jamison ran behind her yelling,

"WAIT FO ME GAL!....wants to be round when ya' tell her, jus' in case I needs to make it plain ."

They both walked fast through the fields, talking and eating their apples along the way. They walked so fast until they almost ran out of breathe.They arrived to the Plantation house moments later and walk into the kitchen. They found Gladdia standing at the stove, stirring a pot while Ola was cutting vegetables. Annabelle walked over near the table and sat the bucket of apples on the floor; she began to help Ola. Gladdia looked over her shoulders toward Annabelle,

"Sho' takes ya long enough gal!...gots to help me wit dese pies and preserves fo' massa git back here."

Annabelle was so excited to tell Gladdia about her and Jamison's conversation until she could hardly hold it in any longer,
"Mama!...how comes ya never says anything to me bout the nawlf!"

she exclaimed.

Gladdia heard Annabelle's question and instantly her heart began to beat at a fast pace. Fear over-powered her mind and she could hardly think clearly. She stopped stirring the pot, turned her head toward Jamison and gave him a disappointed look; assuming that he was responsible for Annabelle's question.

Gladdia had heard many things about the North. She has seen many Slaves get punished and killed for even uttering the word from their mouth. She vowed when Annabelle was a baby, to never allow her to find out about such a place, for fear of her getting into trouble.

She left the stove and walked over to Annabelle, making sure that she stood directly in front of her.

"You mind yo' mouf gal!"

she spoke harshly,

"Miss Patterson or the massa hears ya' speaking anything bout the nawlf....and dey hangs you and me both....spose massa Jamison here tells ya all bout it!"

Jamison began to speak on Annabelle's behalf, he loved her and did not want Gladdia to be upset over an idea that he put into her head,

"I tells Anna bout it Gladdie."

He said calmly,

"See my uncle McAuthor moved dere to do a service fo' God...be a preacher! The day before he leave he tell me all bout it....and well uhm....I tells Anna."

The kitchen became quiet; Ola heard the entire conversation but did not say a word to anyone. Gladdia felt that Annabelle had a right to know the truth. She decided at that moment to confirm Jamison's story. She walked back over to the stove and began stirring in the pot,
"Nawlf be a place where slavery not exist."

She said in a low tone,

"Everyone is free to be whatever dey wants to be…..it be a place only us can dream about, cause all dat try to git dere ends up dead fo' dey arrive. Be's far away from here chile and hard to git dere so I's keep it from my mind, and ya best to keep it far from ya own!"

Gladdia stopped stirring for a moment and looked straight ahead. Tears began to build in her eyes. It was her and Beauford's dream for Annabelle to one day make it to the North and be exposed to a better life, but she felt that now was not the time for her. She needed to be older and have better knowledge of the life she lived. Gladdia had to protect her at all costs.

"Must forget all bout the nawlf right now chile."

Gladdia explained,

"Forget massa Jamison tells ya anything bout it!....most Slaves die jus' for speakin on it!"

Gladdia began stirring the pot again, Annabelle continued to interject,

"But mama!...massa McAuthor say we all be free one day, free to love who we want, and be who we want."

Gladdia became frustrated at Annabelle and her eagerness to know more about the North. Although she wanted her to be aware, she did not want her to do anything that may put her life in danger. She felt that she must do something to make certain that she did not dwell on it any longer. Gladdia slammed the spoon down on the stove and ran back over to where Annabelle was sitting. She stiffened her hand and slapped Annabelle hard across her face, so hard until she almost fell from the kitchen chair. Gladdia then spoke to her in a rough tone,

"Don't lemme hear ya speak like dat round here again EVER!..you member one thang chile, we all belongs right here on dis Plantation! Dats the way the good lawd made it!"

Annabelle's eyes filled with tears, not from her mothers' hands, but from the thought of never getting to a place in life where she could be free to live.

As Gladdia stood in front of the stove, she was still angry and disturbed from what had occurred. She looked toward heaven and mumbled these words,

"Loss my husband, not gon' lose my own chile…..go on and finish ya chores gal, go on nah!"

Annabelle looked over at Jamison standing across the room. She quietly rose from the table and left the kitchen. Jamison watched her leave until she was out of his sight. He looked over at Gladdia standing at the stove.

"Go ahead an help her boy!"

 Gladdia said,

"No need in ya sittin here wit us lookin all loss in the head."

Jamison didn't give a reply. He quickly rose from the table and ran off to catch up with Annabelle. Minutes later he found her in the fields hanging white linen on the clothes line.
When he spotted her, he walked toward her and leaned across the clothes line so that they were facing each other. He looked her in the eyes with a sly grin on his face,

"When ya' thank ya' gone be finished hangin out dis linen gal?"

he asked as he looked around at the other full baskets on the ground.

Annabelle took a moment to respond, she was extremely frustrated and didnt feel like talking, yet she was happy that Jamison was with her. She smiled graciously to hide her aggravation.

"Gots a long way to go."

she replied gently,

"Gots to have it all done fo' sunset, so ya best leave me alone."

Jamison knew everything about Annabelle. He recognized when she was prickly or frustrated. He did not like her in that state of mind. He walked closer to her and began to speak teasingly with an even bigger smile than before,

"Spose when ya' done, ya' wouldn't wanna go pickin berries and sit under the fig tree wit me, now would ya gal!"....

Annabelle continued to hang linen. Even though a big part of her wanted to leave that basket along with her frustrations and run off with him to pick berries, she remembered her obligations and she intended to stick with them,

"Toldya..got dis here linen to hang out and I gots mo' chores round here that need to be done."

she replied regretfully.

Jamison took a look at Annabelle; then observed all of the linen that needed to be hung out on the line. Without asking her for permission, he decided to help her out. They began working together as a team, hanging up the sheets and folding those that were already dry.

Gladdia looked out the kitchen window and observed the both of them working together; she then turned around to face Ola; looking at her in a confused manner,

"Just don't seem natural fo' dat boy to be runnin round wit my baby!...

she said,

"Wonder why he so different from the rest, why he love her much as he do?"

Ola did not respond to Gladdia, she seemed to be disturbed from her inner thoughts. She continued to chop vegetables and listen to Gladdia vent. After a few minutes of listening and voicing her opinion, she layed the knife down on the table and began crying uncontrollably. Gladdia had never seen Ola that upset before. She became frightened and perplexed from her actions,

"Ola gal, what you be cryin for?"

Gladdia asked her excitedly.

Ola sat at the table crying so hard until she had
trouble breathing. After a few seconds of Gladdia's
comfort; she began to explain herself,

"Its my Shadrach, he ran off a few nights ago
headed nawlf!.....say he comes back fo' me. But
jus.....jus dis moanin I hears massa say if dey
catches him, dey beat em' half to death so he wont
run off again!.....What if dey fine him
Gladdie?....What if dey kills my Shadrach?"

  Gladdia began to feel sad for Ola. She sat down
at the table beside her. As she prepared herself to
comfort Ola, she was reminded of her Beauford,
his strength, and his loyalty to the people on the
Plantation; if only he were there to help her
through these hard times. Tears began to fill her
eyes as she layed her hands gently on top of Ola's
to bring comfort to her,

"Shadrach be's a strong man Ola...and if dey do
fine em' I aint never knew fo' a massa to kill his
own slave.....dey needs em' to work the fields....
Lawd he minds me lot of my Beauford!....real
strong man he was."

  Gladdia stood from the kitchen table and
walked toward the window, she looked out at
Annabelle and Jamison; then continued speaking,

"My baby girl..I look at her and I see dat look in
her eyes when she wit dat boy....she done fell
inlove wit em'.....and lovin a white boy gits her in

a heap a trouble in dis world ya' know…..dere be nothin I can do bout it!.....cant stop love from happenin to her."

Ola stood from the table and walked over to Gladdia. She wrapped her arms around her, hugging from the back. They both stood at the window. She whispered to her softly,

"Thinkin maybe he loves her too Gladdie, and he loves her for who SHE be!..and she be GOD'S chile Gladdie! A gift to you, Beauford, and the world…gots to share her Gladdie,… gots to share her wit the world!"

Gladdie listened to Ola and began to cry softly,

 "Ola I's be scared of what the world may do to her…..what will it do to em' both Ola!"

Ola turned Gladdia around to face her; they looked each other in the eyes. The worries of Shadrach and Annabelle overpowered them both; yet Ola gave Gladdia a word of advice and encouragement,

"Good lawd be watchin over dem Gladdie…..both of em'. He wont let nothin happen to em' dats not his will. Ya got to let our chirren be free to learn of dis world fo' demselves…..else dey turn bitter….bitter like ourselves."

Gladdia listened to Ola, took a deep breath to ease her anxiety and walked over toward the stove to finish preparing dinner. As she looked out of the window and gazed at Annabelle and Jamison working in the fields, she was reminded of the day that she gave birth to her.

When her Beauford held Annabelle in his arms for the first time, felt her warmth and smelled her scent, he looked over at Gladdia with tears in his eyes and said,

"She will be strong like roots of an oak tree, and have more than what us have." Those words remain hidden in Gladdia's heart since the day he said them to her.

It was at that moment when she realized that it was time to stop worrying about Annabelle and start holding on to her husbands' word and Gods promise that he made to her. As she looked down into the pot and stirred clockwise, she took one final look out of the window. She looked at her daughter; then over at Ola and responded with immense gratification,

"God tol' me dat my baby,… she be jus fine Ola…..he tol' me that if I jus hol' on to his loving hands, he make sho' my baby be jus fine."

Ola walked over and grabbed Gladdia by the hand. They both agreed that no matter what the situation may have looked like; God said that he would protect her, and they believed it.

After spending over an hour hanging out linen, Annabelle and Jamison were almost finished at that point. Annabelle was more experienced with hanging linen. She finished her bakset before Jamison. However she was eager to lend him a helping hand to help speed up his process. As the two of them continued working, Jamison began to think back on the situation that occurred in the kitchen earlier that day with Gladdia and Annabelle. Although he did not want to mention it again, he couldn't help but wonder to himself, what would cause Gladdia to become so upset about the North.

It was evident from the look on Annabelle's face that she was still upset from the whole ordeal, however; she refused to mention anything to Jamison. Annabelle knew that once he built enough nerve, he would ask her enough questions to get all of the answers he needed. So as they worked on the last basket of linen, making sure that each one was done perfectly, Jamison decided that it was a perfect opportunity to ask Annabelle about Gladdia,

"Why ya reckon Gladdie got so upset bout the North?"
he asked,

"Think she ever wanted to go dere?"

Annabelle walked through the hanging linen to make sure that there weren't any dirt stains on them. Even though she was uncomfortable with the question that Jamison asked her, she felt that she should answer it the best way she knew how,

"Mama say the nawlf be too far to even think about…humph! How she gon' git dere anyway, she cant leave….none of us can! We all belongs to the massa."

Jamison hung the last of the linen on the clothes line, then responded to Annabelle's comment,
 "Well one day I's gonna git dere!...gonna go and find my uncle and git away from all dis hatin goin on round here…and Anna you's comin along wit me!"

     Annabelle smiled big after hearing Jamison's pronouncement, the thought of leaving the Plantation and traveling North with Jamison made her feel happy and anxious all at the same time,

"Well how ya spose we's gittin dere"

 asked Annabelle as she paced through the white linen on the Plantation yard. Jamison began to walk steadily behind her, placing his hands upon her shoulders gently to guide her around the yard,

"Well we jus gon' have to ride on my horse!..papa says I can have one of my own sometime next year…gonna have em' trained special jus for me!"

     Annabelle listened to Jamison boast around the yard while grabbing a sheet of linen from the line and folding it,

"Nah you cut yo foolin round…aint gittin on no horse wit you!...tryin to git us both killed fo' we even make it dere"….

Jamison stood in front of Annabelle as she was folding a sheet and replied,

"I said I's gonna git me a horse to ride off to the North …and you's comin WIT ME!"

Immediately after making that comment to Annabelle, Jamison snatched the sheet from her hands and ran as fast as he could through the fields. He was halfway across the Plantation in less than five minutes. Annabelle ran after him,

"COME BACK HERE JAMISON….YA' BRINGS DAT BACK NAH!"

Annabelle cried out loudly as she limped behind him as fast as she could without falling. They ran across the Plantation fields for nearly ten minutes until they arrived at the old fig tree where they used to sit,

"Look watcha' done….got the sheet all filthy! Nah ima have to wash it over again."

cried Annabelle as Jamison flopped down on the ground under the tree. He smiled and extended his hand to help her sit down beside him.
"Thought you said we was pickin berries….no berries round here!...only figs."

Annabelle said as she positioned herself beside
Jamison on the ground. Jamison took the white
sheet linen and spread it evenly across their legs to
protect them from mosquitos,

"We will."

he replied,

 "Jus stopped here for a lil rest dats all."

Annabelle sighed and leaned over to rest her head
on Jamison's shoulder,

"mama be right mad at me if she finds out im out
here wit you and not tendin to my chores"

she said sadly.

 Jamison grabbed Annabelle's hand and rubbed it
gently,

 "My mama not even know where I be half the
time, and my pa stays gone a lot."

Once Jamison mentioned his father to Annabelle,
she became sad; she never had an opportunity to
develop a relationship with her father, so her
feelings are slightly hurt.

"Wish my pa was still alive."

She said with tears in her eyes,

"My father die when I was jus a little baby, mama say he take his own life cause he didn't believe anymore, she say he was a real good man."

"Well my pa be's alive but I hardly spend time wit him"

replied Jamison,

"he say he rather die than spend all day at home wit mama….I don't even see em' kiss anymore, it's like they hate each other."

Annabelle sat there silently for a moment, enjoying the tingling sensations that slowly crawled up her back from Jamison's hand rubs, suddenly she replied,

"Jamison, ya ever kiss a girl before?....ever wonder what it be like, or what it feel like?"

Jamison became nervous, although he's always dreamed of kissing Annabelle, he never thought that he would have the opportunity. His mother always said that Slaves were like animals and should be treated at such. He continued to rub her hand and responded promptly,

"Well….it be's something that a man and woman do when dey loves each other, mama and papa use to do it a lot when I was little"

Jamison and Annabelle paused and looked each other in the eyes. They became extremely nervous around each other, almost trembling from anticipation. Deep inside they shared a strong love for one another but never knew how to express themselves. Jamison's parents would more than likely have Annabelle and Gladdia beaten to death at even the thought of it, but ironically they found themselves in this secret quandary.

"Reckon I can show ya how its done."
Jamison answered,

"Dat way ya knows what it feels like…dat is if ya wanna try Anna."

Annabelle looked around the fields to make sure no one was around. She took a deep breath,

"Spose I should know what a real kiss should feel like"

she replied,

"Mama kiss me all the time, but I's neva kiss a boy….what I spose to do?"

Jamison slid closer to Annabelle so that there legs were touching one another, his heart began to beat at a faster pace and his palms became sweaty. He paid it no mind. He put his left arm around her shoulders to pull her in closer to him, so close until they could feel each others' warm breathing graze over their lips.

"ya have to make your lips touch mine and sit real close."

he said as he grabbed her hand and looked her deeply in the eyes.

Annabelle began to experience a weird feeling. She became anxious and very warm. She closed her eyes and leaned in closer toward Jamison. As their lips touched one another, it was as if they belonged there, like two magnets drawn to each other. Their eyes remained closed and they kissed each other soft and tenderly, entering into a world where only the two of them existed.

They found themselves lossed in each other, so intrigued by the kiss until they became unaware of the fact that Maryrose and her lady friends were making their evening stroll through the Plantation fields and fastly approaching the two of them. As Maryrose and her company moved in closer and noticed the two of them kissing each other, they became very disturbed, so disturbed until Maryrose screamed to the top of her longs and passed out in front of the fig tree.

Their kiss was interrupted by Maryrose's scream. Jamison and Annabelle quickly rose from the ground, grabbed each other by the hand and ran off into the fields. They left Maryrose with her friends to revive her. Jamison and Annabelle ran as fast as they could, laughing and passing up Slaves who were working in the fields. They approached a pond near the church. Jamison walked toward the pond, Annabelle lingered behind. He motioned for her to come closer.

"Come Anna…don't be afraid, wont let nothin happen to ya."

Even though Annabelle had complete trust in Jamison, she was terrified of being close to the water.

"I never been dat close to the water before."

she said,

"mama tells me of a Slave who died in dere a while ago."

"Well dontcha come out here wit the church from time to time?"

Jamison asked as he stood there, appearing confused.

"A few people come out here wit the preacher fo church service."

Annabelle explained,

"Dey gives there life to God here….I think about doin it myself, but I's be afraid… think about dat Slave who died."

Jamison grabbed Annabelle by the hand and motioned for her to sit with him alongside the pond.

"Ya need not to be afraid Anna"

he explained,

"Ya see my uncle tells me dat dis here pond is a special pond…it has POWERS!…its touched by God, and if ya ever feelin bad, or hurtin inside….ya jus come down here and git in the pond and wash it all away, God's power washes away the pain."

Annabelle began to wave her feet in the water, "Never heard nothin like dat before."

she replied,

"Reckon it work for Slaves too?"

Jamison put his feet in the water and began to rub them gently against Annabelles'

"My uncle says it works for anyone who needs a touch from God."

he explained,

"Says sometimes bad feelings and pain be jus like dirt, and ya needs a special place to go and wash it off to feel clean……..welp! guess we best git up from here and head home, reckon everyone is lookin for us by now."

Annabelle and Jamison rose up from the ground and began to walk slowly toward the Plantation house, holding each other by the hand.

When they finally arrived, they walked in the house together through the back kitchen entrance. They found Gladdia and Ola sitting at the table appearing upset, Annabelle and Jamison stood their holding hands.

"Good day Gladdie and Ola."

said Jamison, as he stood there with a smile on his face.

"Today be's a BAD day."

replied Gladdie in a sad tone,

"A BAD day fo the both of ya!...Miss Patterson be's upstairs wantin to see ya right nah Anna, she be right mad at what ya done out dere wit Massa Jamison…..best go on up dere and see what she wonts wit ya!...she fussed at me badly and tol me to go find ya. Only pray she sho ya some mercy chile….go on nah!"

Annabelle looked at Jamison. She left the kitchen and slowly walked up the staircase that led to Maryrose's bedroom. As she was walking up slowly, she became frightened. Her stomach had a weird feeling and her hands were trembling.

She had witnessed more than a few Slaves who had received hard punishment on the Plantation. She wondered if this would be the day that she is given hers. Was she wrong for kissing Jamison underneath the fig tree? These questions she asked herself as she slowly made her way to the bedroom.

As she walked into the room, she found Maryrose standing near the window awaiting her arrival. She turned to face Annabelle as she stood near the bedroom door. Her arms were folded and her legs were trembling from fear of what would happen next.

"Don't you stand dere tryin to look like Miss innocent!"

cried Maryrose,

"I know what ya did and I sent for ya to come and take ya
punishment!"

Annabelle began to fidget with her hands from nervousness, tears built in her eyes,

"But Miss Patterson, I's not do nothin wrong ma'am!"

she replied.

Maryrose walked over to Annabelle and began yelling at the top of her lungs,

"YOU PUT YO BLACK MOUF ON MY BOY AND YOU ARE GONNA PAY FO WHAT YOU DID TO HIM AND TO ME!"

At this point, Annabelle assumed that she was about to receive a whipping. She began to prepare herself by slowly removing her Plantation dress. She continued to explain herself,

"Miss Patterson!....I....I done nothin wrong ma'am....pleeeeease!"
 cried Annabelle,
    Maryrose was not inspired by her plea, she grabbed a small whip; yet big enough to bring a human to its knees. She held it firmly in her hands. Maryrose stood in front of Annabelle, who was completely naked and began yelling at her louder than before,

"NOTHING WRONG!...YOU SAID YOU DID NOTHING WRONG!"

    Maryrose became more upset and aggravated. Without any more delays, she walked behind Annabelle and began whipping her across the back. She gave her more than ten lashes and yelled the word "liar" between each one. The lashes were so hard and severe until they ripped pieces of her flesh, causing her to cry out in agony.

Gladdia, Ola; along with Jimmy and Jamison remained downstairs in the living area, pacing the floor from nervousness. Annabelle's crying was so strong and intense until they heard her clearly from upstairs. Gladdia and Jamison stood their silently and cried for her.

As Gladdia paced the floor with tears falling from her eyes, she began to pray for her daughter; asking God to keep his arms of protection around her and to heal her heart of any hatred that may develop from this trauma. It was her belief that Slave owners only beat their slaves because it was what they were taught and that only prayer could change their hearts.

Even though her daughters punishment caused her to have a bourdened heart; she took joy in knowing that one day Daniel and Maryrose would have to answer to God for their behavior towards Slavery, and their lack of respect toward negroes.

Later on that night, Gladdia and Big Debra gathered around the pond with other Slaves to sing gospel spirituals with one another. It was their intent to rid the land of death and evil spirits. They offered special prayers for Shadrach, Annabelle, and those who were suffering from illnesses. Praying together before going to sleep would bring peace within the Quarters, helping them to forget about their hardships and to rest easy during the night.

Early the next morning, Gladdia, Annabelle; along with Ola and Hattie walked through the Slave Quarters toward the Plantation house for work. As they shared a conversation together, they noticed a horse and covered wagon parked out in front of the house with a Caucasian driver. Annabelle smiled to herself with excitement, it was her prayer that McAuthor would come back to the Plantation to be with them; maybe this was God answering her prayer.

They all stop speaking and slowed down to observe the situation. The front door opened with Maryrose, Daniel and Jamison carrying out traveling bags; no McAuthor was in site. As they all walked down the porch steps, Jamison looked out into the fields and recognize Annabelle. He stared at her until he reached the wagon. They positioned all the traveling bags into the wagon; Maryrose and Daniel watched Jamison as he climbed on board.

The driver then began driving away with Jamison. He and Annabelle stared at one another until the wagon disappeared into the trees. Annabelle's eyes filled with tears. She wondered where they sent him and would he ever return to the Plantation. Gladdia, Ola and Hattie just shook their heads slowly and proceeded to walk toward the house. Annabelle stood there in disbelief, staring at the trees.

"Best c'mon chile!"

 yelled Gladdia as she looked back at Annabelle standing there with her feet firmly planted to the ground. Gladdia stood in one spot and waited for her to catch up. Once they began walking beside each other Annabelle began crying even harder.

"Stop all that cryin chile, ya learn to git use to it after a while."

replied Gladdia,

"he wont know ya when he come back…he wont know ya at all."

VI

Annabelle and Eliza were busy cleaning the living area. Eliza was dusting the furniture and Annabelle was down on her hands and knees scrubbing the floors. It had been four years since Jamison's departure. The girls were now seventeen years old and had become permanent house servants. Gladdia was still the main cook.

"Mighty quiet dere Anna…something troubling ya?"

asked Eliza as she looked down at Annabelle on the floor.

"Reckon I's be alright."

she replied,
"Lots a thinkin I been doin is all….sometime I wish I could jus talk to my pa…even tho I neva met em'….maybe he could help me figure a few thangs out if he be alive rite nah."

Eliza just nodded her head in agreement and continued to dust the furniture. Annabelle stopped cleaning the floor for a moment, looked around to make sure that no one was coming into the room. She asked Eliza a question,

"Ever git tide a being a Slave….workin here an cookin all day?"

Eliza stopped dusting and looked at Annabelle in disbelief. Although she hate being a Slave, she always thought it was best to keep her feelings to herself.

"Mama says we all belongs right here!"

Eliza replied,

"The good lawd put us all here fo a reason."

Annabelle became frustrated with Eliza's comment. She arose from the floor and walked over toward her. She snatched the dust cloth from her hands,

"Good lawd not intend fo' us to be here on dis Plantation and suffer NO!...he wants us to live in peace, to love one anotha an to be happy."

Annabelle tossed the cloth back to Eliza and walked over toward the window to fiddle around with the drapes for a few seconds. She then turned around swiftly, looked over at Eliza, and spoke softly,

"LIZA....did you know dere is a place on the otha side of the Mississippi up nawlf called Canada?....where niggras, and whites all live togetha. No slavery, no beatings...no hangins!"

Eliza looked around the room to make sure that no one was entering. She walked over swiftly toward Annabelle and spoke in a low tone, "Mama say not to listen to ya when ya talking fool like dis!......say only place dat be peaceful is heaven, no otha place round here like dat gal!"

Annabelle grabbed Eliza by the hand and pulled her closer. She looked her straight in the eyes,

"Be knowin what I's talkin bout gal…..come!....I's show ya!"

Annabelle grabbed Eliza by the hand and dragged her out the front door and into the storage shed out back. They walked into the shed and sat down on a haystack. Annabelle began to explain,

"Be's a while ago when he tells me, was only like twelve or thirteen, he say his uncle tell him bout a place called Canada, it be's up nawlf…it……it be a place where ya' scape to be free!...he say errybody be's equal Liza!...school fo the colored people, work, …..he say he take me wit em'…but deys sent em' away"

Eliza sat on the haystack in front of Annabelle and looked at her with concern,

"Whose ya talking bout Anna?....whose gon' come an take ya away?"

she asked.

Annabelle stood from the haystack and walked toward the wall. She turned around and looked at Eliza,

"Ya be's my friend LIZA?"

she asked,

"Why yessum!"

Eliza replied,

"Ya be's the ONLY friend I got!"

Annabelle walked into the door entrance of the shed and looked out into the yard,

"His name be's Jamison"

she said,

"The massa's boy?"

asked Eliza.

Annabelle turned from the entrance to face Eliza, she replied as if she were trying to convince a confused jury,

"He's nothin like dem....he tells me errythang bout Canada...say his uncle be's dere waitin for em'. He tol' me he would take me away wit em but dey sends em away few years ago. Ya remember Liza?....dey send em away cause dey know....deys know the whole time Liza!"

"I remember how the two of ya would always be togetha...even at church."

said Eliza,

"Could barely keep ya apart from each otha…what ya figure dey knows bout em Anna?....why deys send em away for?"

"Cause dey know he loves me!"

replied Annabelle,

"And I love him!.....good lawd put us together and dey sent em away is what dey did!........prays to the lawd to send em back to me….I's feel empty inside, like parts a me die off when he leave. Looks at the sky at night and I wonders to myself if he eva think bout me."

Annabelle turned around toward the storage entrance and looked out into the yard once more,

"There's a life fo' me in Canada…and one day ima fine it!"
Eliza listened to Annabelle closely; although she was scared to hear her speak that way, deep inside she believed every word. She stood from the haystack and walked over to her. She put her arms around her shoulder with a smile on her face,

"Best fine our way back to cleanin…else ya dreamin git us beat fo' we even has a chance to see dis here LIFE ya speaks so proud bout gal!"

Annabelle looked at Eliza and smiled,

"Oh gal! cut ya worries, we's headed back right nah!"

she replied.

Annabelle grabbed Eliza by the hand and proceeded toward the Plantation house. As they were walking with each other, they ran into Eliza's older brother and house servant Jimmy,

"Knew I heard noises comin from out here!"

he announced,

"You gals ought to be in the house tendin to ya chores, not playin round out chere!.....massa be's right mad to catch ya....specially YOU Liza, massa was kind enuff to brang ya out the fields and dis the thanks you give em!"

"Us jus leavin."

cried Eliza as she grabbed Annabelle by the hand.

As the three of them were making there way to the Plantation house, they stumbled upon Maryrose, she looked at the girls; then at Jimmy,

"Well... what you gals doin out here?.... should be tendin to ya chores!"
Annabelle and Eliza held their heads down, they were too nervous to come up with an excuse,

however; Jimmy mediated the conversation quite well,

"Was jus walkin em back to the house ma'am… had to show em where's we be keepin the Brandy ma'am… incase we need mo' for company."

"Very good Jimmy!..very good!"

said Maryrose,

"Now you girls hurry back to your chores…. lots a work to be done round here…hurry now!"

The girls quickly made their way to the Plantation house.Maryrose and Jimmy watched them as they disappeared.

"Glad you're out here Jimmy"

Maryrose said in a sweet tone,

"Need ya to go back with me to the shed for a moment, come now."

    Jimmy followed Maryrose to the shed, once they arrive; Jimmy walked in and stood beside the window. She walked in behind him.

 "Sit down Jimmy…needs to talk to ya."

demanded Maryrose as she began pacing back and forth on the grassy floors with her hands on her hips.

"Guess ya wonder why I asked ya to come in here wit me Jimmy."

she asked as Jimmy sat down on the haystack looking confused and feeling awkward.

"Thought did cross my mind ma'am,"

replied Jimmy,
"Somethin I can do fo ya ma'am?"

Maryrose slowly walked toward the entrance of the shed and looked out into the fields, she began to speak in a low calm voice,

"Once was a beautiful young lady, who lived on a Slave plantation…jus like this one…she had everything she ever dreamed of…a beautiful son, a nice home…cept' one thang…she had a husband who dint enjoy making love to her…he found more pleasure in a winch slave!.....ohhhhhhh…could ya imagine the hurt and pain that young, sweet, beautiful lady felt?"…..

Jimmy just sat there, with a blank stare in his eyes Maryrose turned from the entrance and walked over to where he sat. She placed her hands over his shoulders and began to rub his chest firmly. She continued with her story,

"Wasn't long for she started wonderin…what would it be like to make love to a Slave of her own…her very own Slave…what…what was so special bout it…. hmm?...what was so special and who would she choose for this secret love affair?"

Jimmy became uneasy and nervous. He stood from the haystack and quickly walked toward the front entrance,

"Gots a lot of work dat needs to be done ma'am"

he replied nervously.

"NOT SO FAST JIMMY BOY!"

Maryrose yelled firmly,

"sit down Jimmy…SIT DOWN NOW!"

He slowly turned from the entrance and walked over to the haystack. As he sat down; Maryrose walked over to him and continued to rub on his chest. She spoke calmly to him, in a seductive manner,

"Who would she choose?"
Maryrose asked,

"There was only one Slave on the Plantation who caught her attention…..was the one her husband trusted the most…his most loyal servant was the one she chose."

"Couldn't do no such a thang!"….cried Jimmy,

"Massa would kill me ma'am!"

Maryrose leaned over his shoulder and began to whisper in his ear in a cunningly fashion,

"You will…or I promise ya Jimmy, bad things will happen to you and your family….Slaves not have much say so on this Plantation…no matta how long ya been here…ya still jus a nigger!"

Maryrose began pacing the floor arrogantly, her power of persuasion slowly convinced Jimmy to consider her deceitful plans,

"Master at the Richmond Plantation be lookin for a strong young gal like Eliza!"

she explained deviously,

"Daniel been thinkin bout selling her….but I can make sho' she stays put….would ya like dat Jimmy?....wanna keep ya family together don't'cha?…poor Big Debra would be sooooo upset!"

She walked over to Jimmy and kneeled down in front of him, she slowly un-buttoned his shirt and began to kiss him passionately on his chest, then she began to whisper real seductively,

"Wont let nothin happen to ya Jimmy"

she whispered softly,

"It be our own lil secret....our own lil secret."

Jimmy sat on the haystack while Maryrose kissed and undressed him. He tried with all of his might to resist temptation but was not strong enough. Maryrose's soft wet lips and sweet smelling perfume began to arouse Jimmy and after a while, he found himself wanted her more and more. His hormones began to rage out of control, he was a virgin and in-experienced with women.

As Maryrose gradually moved from his chest up to his lips, he slowly responded by kissing her back, the more they kissed each other, the more passion fabricated between the both of them. Jimmy looked Maryrose in the eyes and undressed her slowly; kissing her on the neck and gently rubbing his hands on her back. Maryrose's hormones danced all over her body as he gently touched her with his strong, hard working hands. Jimmy removed his trousers and layed her down on the grass. As he positioned himself on top of her he could feel her body heat surface through the pores.

He slowly put himself inside of her. Although the size of his erect penis caused her to feel slightly uncomfortable, her body responded immediately and hungered for more; and he obliged. She grabbed on to him tightly and enjoyed every moment of him sliding in and out of her soul. His hard body and aggressiveness intrigued her as they made love unhurriedly. They look each other in the eyes, kissed each other passionately and forgot all about their surroundings. Remarkably, they provided each other with something that was missing from both of their lives; PASSION. The two of them shared a special moment of pleasure, and it was their own little secret.

While Jimmy and Maryrose were in the shed with one another, Annabelle and Eliza worked on their chores together in the dining area.

"I's not know why we has to set all dis silver down on the table for."

said Eliza,

"All it takes is one piece a silver to eat food...humph!...seems to me like dey ask for all dese dishes and silver jus to keep us mo busy cleanin it afta supper!"

Annabelle heard Eliza, but did not respond. Her mind was filled with so many different thoughts and ideas until it caused her to remain speechless, somehow; they over-powered her. Eliza became slightly frustrated by this. She felt as if she were talking to herself in the room. Inspite of the silence, she continued to vent her frustrations,

"Mama say the massa not be satisfied less his Slaves be workin dere fingers to death!...jus the otha day, I lay down a heap a silver and dishes, but only half of it git used!!!!...Miss Patterson make Ola wash every one cause she say dat Slaves carry diseases.....ANNA YOU HEARING ME GAL!!"

Annabelle stopped setting the table, looked up at Eliza, and walked into the kitchen. Eliza followed behind her. When they arrived, they found Ola sitting at the table, stitching on a pillow. Gladdia was busy washing pots and pans in the sink. They all over-heard Eliza yelling Annabelle's name across the kitchen, following behind her and begging for her response.

They both made their way back to the dining area, Eliza continued to yell out Annabelle's name for about five minutes and there was no response. Finally, she grabbed Annabelle by her right hand and turned her around.

"Anna!...whats troubling you gal!"

cried Eliza.

Annabelle slammed the serving spoon on the dining room table and replied,

"Jus aint right Liza....dey beat us round here like we animals....dey has their way wit us. Make our people work all day in the sum wit no food sometimes. Give us babies....sell us off...make our men feel less than nothing, and worst of all, dey not even care bout what dey doin....what us gone do Liza?....how can we ever survive on this here Plantation dis way?"

"Same as our mama and papi did."

said Eliza,

"We do as we tol' round here so dat we can make it through hard times.... we's pray for God to send us a miracle for we dies here.....we look to the stars at night and believe dat one day, dis all be over and maybe we all even be free!"

Annabelle listened to Eliza and instantly began daydreaming about her life of freedom. She dreamed about Jamison and how happy the two of them would have been if he were still there on the Plantation. Before she had an opportunity to respond to Eliza, Maryrose stormed into the dining area from the storage shed, interrupting their conversation,

"Howdy....howdy...howdy."

she said happily to the girls as they diligently worked on their chores. Annabelle and Eliza did not greet her verbally; instead, they smiled warmly and continued with their work.

"Table looks lovely girls….such a wonderful day isn't it?"

Maryrose asked, as she pranced around the dining area like a young school girl.

She stopped and fundled around with the table cloths and settings, then walked toward the dining room entrance,

"Spose I should wash up for dinner."

she said calmly as she looked into the living area and rubbed her fingers through her hair,

"Imagine Daniel will be returning soon….make sure the silver isn't dull girls and be sure to light the candles wont you?"

As Maryrose left the dining area, Annabelle and Eliza just looked at one another in a confused manner and giggled softly.

"What ya reckon git into Miss Patterson…what got her in such a good mood?"
asked Eliza.

"Mama tells me not to speak on such thangs!"

replied Annabelle,

" It be's a dead possum on the roof and I smell it!"

The two of them began giggling softly to one another; suddenly Jimmy walked in. They nudged one another to silence the laughter. Annabelle greeted him in a teasingly manner,

"Howdy-doo Jimmy!"

she said, as Eliza held her head down to suppress the laughter.

"Uhm howdy-doo…..howdy-doo Anna!"

Jimmy answered nervously as he grab an apple from
the kitchen table and quickly made his way toward the dining room entrance. Annabelle and Eliza giggled much louder as he left the room suspiciously,

"Reckon dat be the dead Possum you be speaking of"

said Eliza.

They giggled more with each other, then suddenly they were interrupted by a loud disturbance coming from the kitchen. They ran in quickly to investigate.
Annabelle and Eliza ran into the kitchen and found Gladdia passed out on the floor with Jimmy and Ola leaning over her.

"Good lawd!...what has happened?"

cried Annabelle as her and Eliza kneeled down over her.

"We was gettin supper ready to put out!"

explained Ola,

"Then all a sudden she say she was feelin light-headed…like she couldn't see straight, den- down she went to the flo'…..Jimmy?...what ya reckon wrong wit her?"

Jimmy stood there with a perplexed look on his face. Deep inside he was worried for Gladdia, yet he worked hard to remain calm for the sake of Annabelle and Eliza, who panicked easily. He leaned over Gladdia and called out to her,

"Gladdie!......Gladdie gal!....if ya hears me! den say somethin to me gal!"

Gladdie continued to lay on the floor, with no response. Jimmy looked over at Annabelle, who was holding hands with Eliza. She appeared to be worried.

"She been sick any?"

he asked.

"Aint been sleeping much."

she replied,

"Spends a lot of time up at night; prayin,…sometimes she be up the whole night!"

Eliza walked over to the corner of the room, while the others stood close by. She grabbed a bucket of water near the corner of the sink and threw it on Gladdia's face.

"I remember mama doin dis when Vynna pass out in the fields."

said Eliza,

"Figure it work jus as good on Gladdie."

They all looked down at Gladdia on the floor. To everyone's surprise, the water worked. She layed still with her eyes wide opened.

"Mama!....you be's alright?....can ya git up?"

asked Annabelle.

"Feels a lil dizzy" said Gladdia, "Jimmy! ..will ya help me up from here?"

Annabelle, Ola and Jimmy helped Gladdie from the floor. Eliza pulled a chair from the table. They placed her there gently. Afterward, Annabelle walked swiftly to the kitchen sink to wet a cloth rag. She placed it on Gladdia's forehead. Everyone stood around to examine her reactions. Maryrose walked into the kitchen unexpectedly during the commotion. She looked over at Gladdia sitting there.

"What's the matter wit Gladdie?"

Maryrose asked,

"She took sick?"

"She blacked out ma'am."

replied Ola,

"she be right tide….not much rest dese days."

Annabelle felt bad for her mother. It bothered her to see her in that way. Although Maryrose had a cold heart for Slaves, and hardly ever allowed them to leave early of their household chores, Annabelle felt it was necessary to ask of her mercy,

"Ma'am if ya allow my mama to rest up, I fill-in for her round here…make sho' all work is cared for….sho' Liza be willing to help."

Eliza looked at Annabelle, then at Maryrose and nodded her head in agreement. Maryrose did not give a response immediately. She put her hand on her hips and paced the kitchen floor for a few seconds.

"Well I suppose it be alright!"

she said,

"But ya must do all your chores and hers!...no excuses gal!"

Annabelle looked at her mother sitting there. She could tell from the look in her eyes that she was overworked and extremely exhausted. She grabbed her hand and rubbed it gently to bring comfort,

"Yes ma'am, I swear to it."

said Annabelle

.

Maryrose ordered Jimmy to escort Gladdia to the Quarters. She also gave orders to Annabelle and Eliza, instructing them to clean the kitchen and to help Ola with dinner. She stormed out of the kitchen and into the living area to prepare a glass of red wine for relaxation. Jimmy helped Gladdia from the chair by putting her arm around his shoulders. They slowly walked out the back door and headed for the Quarters.

As Jimmy and Gladdia were walking through the Quarters toward her cabin, Big Debra noticed them walking and ran over to their rescue.

"Jimmy!....what done happened to her?"

she cried.

"I's be fine gal….jus needs a lil rest is all."

Gladdia said as she balanced her weight on Jimmy's shoulders.

"Blacked out in the kitchen is what she did back dere"

Jimmy said to Big Debra as she stood in front of them with her hands on her wide hips, looking bewildered. She then walked over to the other side of Gladdia and put her arms around her so that there was a smooth balance between her and Jimmy.

"Well lemme help ya to the cabin!"

Big Debra said eagerly,

"Declares the massa will workya til ya falls DEAD!"
"Aint quite dead yet!"

 cried Gladdia as she walked slowly with Jimmy and Big Debra toward her cabin,

 "Spose God got mo' for me round here….guess dis his way a lettin me know I needs a good restin!"

They walked a few more minutes until they arrived at the cabin. Once they walked in and enter the bedroom, Jimmy positioned Gladdia in her bed. She layed there peacefully while Big Debra sat on the edge of the bed.

"Dere now!..ya jus lay here and git plenty a rest, Anna and Liza takes care a everythang for ya back at the house!"

Gladdia layed there and thought about all of the household chores and responsibilities that she left behind; Maryrose and Daniel were hard Slave owners and very hard to satisfy. She began to worry for Annabelle and Eliza.

"Reckon if I git rested up, I can start on those apple pies fo' Miss Patterson tomorrow!"

she said.

Big Debra just looked down at her, smiled and shook her head slowly,

"The Mistress jus may need to be makin her own apple pies, cause you lookin mighty tide up in here gal....mighty tide indeed!"

She pulled the sheet over Gladdia's legs and secured her in the bed tightly. Jimmy stood alongside the bed, looking down at them both with a gentle smile on his face.

"Well me and Jimmy best be goin' now, I gots to finish up a lil more in the fields before sun down."

said Big Debra as she kissed Gladdia on the forehead.

"Yea, the master not like me bein' away from the house too long."
said Jimmy,

"He say a house nigger should always stay PUT!"

As they were beginning to walk out the door, Jimmy offered to walk his mother to the sugarcane fields but she declined, saying that she could manage just fine without him. She reassured Gladdia that she would return the next morning to check on her. Although Gladdia was feeling very worn-out and also worried for Annabelle having an extra load of chores, she was very confident that everything would be okay and that God would take care of everything. Jimmy and Big Debra left the cabin; Gladdia layed alone in the bed. She thought of all the things that she had went through from the moment that Annabelle was born. She looked beyond her ceiling and imagined that she was looking toward heaven.

Gladdia did something that she had never done before, she said a special prayer for Maryrose and Daniel, although they spent years being cruel to her and the other Slaves on the Plantation, she realized that it had to be something that it was a sickness. She felt a strong need to pray for their souls, and to also ask God to remove any hatred or unforgiveness from her heart. Afterward, she dwelled on nothing but happy thoughts and fell soundly to sleep.

Later on that night, while Gladdia was back at the cabin sleeping; Annabelle and Eliza were busy clearing the dining room table. As Maryrose and Daniel sat there wiping their mouths and sipping on lemonade, they complimented Annabelle on how well she prepared the food. Annabelle was extremely flattered, however; she did not accept the recognition. She understood that it was her mother who worked all evening preparing the food. She insisted that all admiration go to her. As they continued to clear the table of all dirty dishes and silver, Maryrose walked to the bar to prepare another glass of Brandy

"Slow down Mary!"

Daniel said,

"Not good for a lady to drink too much and go over her limit."

He was aware that Maryrose enjoyed drinking alcohol and tended to become intoxicated and provoke arguments. He did not want to open the door for any disagreements. Daniel arose from the table and walked over toward the sofa to relax while lighting his smoking pipe.

"Where is Gladdie?"

he asked,

"Shouldn't she be here wit' the others?...havent seen her since early today."

Maryrose had feelings of revulsion whenever Daniel mentioned Gladdia's name, however; she maintained her composure well enough to enjoy her glass of Brandy,

"Sent her to the Quarters early."

she replied,

"She took sick and fell-out in the kitchen, tide I guess....although I couldn't imagine why....she hardly does any work round here."

Annabelle overheard Maryrose's comment regarding Gladdia's sickness and became upset. Daniel noticed the mean look that appeard on her face, however; Eliza pulled her into the kitchen before he could say anything to her about it.

"Reckon I go down to the Quarters before I leave for Mississippi tomorrow."
Daniel said,

"Gonna take her some medicine and herbs to git her well...cant have one of my house winches down and out during this season."

At that moment, Maryrose was on her third glass of Brandy, and was beginning to experience a mild case of intoxication. She walked over to

Daniel and stood in front of him while he sat on the sofa smoking his pipe.

"We wouldn't want anything to happen to that GLADDIE of yours….now would we!"

Maryrose said in a sarcastic tone. She slammed her empty glass down on the coffee table and continued,

"Why dontcha' jus move her in here for GOOD!"

Daniel could sense that Maryrose had become intoxicated. He was irritated with her disposition. He slammed his pipe down on the table, stood up and grabbed her by the arms. Without hesitation, he started shaking her intensely and yelling at her,

"WHAT IN TORNATION HAS GOTTEN INTO YOU GAL…..CANT TALK TO ME THAT WAY…I WILL HAVE ORDER!!!....YOU UNDERSTAND ME GAL!!"

Maryrose allowed Daniel to yell at her without reprisal. She snatched away from him and staggered toward the staircase showing no remorse for his feelings,

"I'm goin to bed Daniel."

she said calmly,

"Give my regards to your BED WHORE!"

She proceeded to walk up the staircase toward her bedroom. Daniel became furious at her response but refused to say anything. He picked up the drinking glass from the table, threw it down and shattered it on the floor. He sat down on the sofa to calm himself while Annabelle and Eliza continued to clear the dining area.

They worked together on every task, making sure that everything was done perfectly. Within an hour, all of their chores were completed. They offered to assist Ola with her duties, but she refused. She rather spend time alone in the main house, talking to God and saying special prayers for the Slaves on the Plantation. Soon Annabelle and Eliza were leaving Ola to herself. Ola made sure that everything in the kitchen was cleaned properly and placed in its rightful area before she returned to the Quarters. Ola and Gladdia resembled each other. They were both systematic hard workers.

As Ola completed her household chores and headed toward the Quarters, she began to experience awkward feelings in her stomach, not a sick feeling, but more of a fearful feeling, as if something strange were about to occur. She began singing gospel hymns to herself, focusing on the lyrics that usually helped to ease her mind.

As she approached her cabin, she observed a well-dressed gentleman wearing a hat, sitting on her porch in an old chair. Who was this man? And why was he dressed so fancy. The closer she moved toward the cabin, the more she began to recognize exactly who that man was; it was her

Shadrach, her husband who left the Plantation,
seeking his freedom over three years ago.
Ola walked toward him. He slowly stood up from
that old rusted chair on the porch and ran swiftly
toward her.

"Shadrach!....good lawd!"

cried Ola as she ran toward him. Tears filled both
of their eyes like and overflowing dam as Shadrach
grabbed Ola and spun her around in his arms. He
positioned her on the ground to stand in front of
him. He greeted her warmly with a slow and
passionate kiss to the lips.

"Thought dey killed ya!....thought I would neva
see ya again."

Ola said calmly as she embraced the right side of
his face with her hand.
    Shadrach took her hand, and led her inside of
the cabin. Once they walked in, Ola slowly walked
over to the corner of the room. She stood there
with her head held down and arms folded.
Shadrach looked across the room at her. She was
as beautiful as she was three years ago when he
left the Plantation. He walked behind and pulled
her in close to him.

"Toldya I's comin back fo' ya gal…made it all the
way nawlf I did…and I's back here to take ya
back wit me!"

As Ola listened to him make his declaration to her, she felt herself becoming skeptical and scared. She made up in her mind years ago that her Shadrach was gone and never coming back. She considered the fact that she would probably die on that Plantation, never becoming a free woman. Years had passed and Ola was now weak and tired, traveling north would be too much for her to handle.

"What about work…and…and…and where's we gone live?"
said Ola.

Shadrach turned her around to face him,

"Got me a job workin down at the cotton mill."

he said proudly.

"Cant say it pay much, but it be's an honest wage fo us……ole man Prentis says he put us up at his cabin til we git somethin of our own."

Shadrach smiled at Ola as he proudly explained to her his plans and accomplishments. Ola walked toward the bed and sat on the edge. She looked up at him with tears building in her eyes.

"Cant leave wit you Shadrach."

she said sadly,

" Ya Been gon' a while nah……..I be's tide, I would only git in the way….dey catch us if I come along!"

Shadrach looked at Ola in disbelief, she was behaving much differently than what he expected. He walked in front of her and kneeled down on the un-even floors. He grabbed her by the hand and looked her in the eyes, at that point, his only hope was to beg her for reconsideration.

"OLA!....ya' gots to come back wit me."

he said,

"Ya' all I got in dis world. My ma and papi be's gone long time ago. Wit out cha I'm nothin….you be's the only reason why I leaves for the nawlf Ola!....I worked hard gal…I worked hard to keep my promise to ya..and I comes here to take ya from all dis hate and evil here!.....ya deserves a much betta life, and I's gon' give it to ya……ya comin wit me gal?"….

Ola looked up toward the ceiling. The tears began to burn her eyes as they ran slowly down the sides of her face. She looked down at her Shadrach, sitting on his knees. His eyes were full of hope, motivation and encouragement. She no longer possessed those qualities. She allowed herself to become confined to Slavery mentality. Ola was content with her life on the Plantation,

"This hear place be's the only place I knows"

 said Ola,

"I knew one day you come back for me…even tho'
I tries to fo'git bout it….but through the years I
grew tide and weary Shadrach!.....not strong, not
strong as you!....rather die here knowin' dat you in
a betta place, livin a betta life…..I cant go bak wit
ya Shadrach."

    Shadrach looked at Ola and layed his head on
her lap, he began to cry for her. They both
understood in their minds that this was a final
goodbye for the both of them. Ola cried and gently
rubbed the side of Shadrach's head,

    "I Wont holdya back from the life ya' always
wanted."

 she said sadly,

 "But I be's right proud of ya'…. ya be's a man
Shadrach!....ya be's a man, and I pray that God
protect ya wit his love. Go Shadrach…..go and
never come back for me again!"

Shadrach began to cry harder, so hard until his
tears caused wet stains in her field dress. He called
out her name repeatedly as if she were beyond his
reach.
Ola took her finger and lifted Shadrach's chin.
Throughout their entire marriage, she had never

experienced him being this upset about anything, unless it was an unjust beating. As she lifted his chin and lookd him closely in his eyes, she spoke to him in a clear voice, almost sounding like a preacher,

"Got put his spirit in ya."

she said,

"Stand STRONG, jus as he is. Be MIGHTY, jus as he is. POWERFUL, just as he is, and mo matta what may come ya way....NEVER STOP FIGHTING!! And NEVER STOP BELIEVING".

They both stood from the bed and held one another tightly. Shadrach kissed Ola passionately, then removed a handkerchief from his back pocket and gave it to her. As he grabbed his luggage bag and looked out the side window for bounty hunters, he quickly ran out of the front door toward the wooded area. Ola looked out of her back window and watched him disappear into the trees. She walked over to the bed and slowly positioned herself there, crying and holding the handkerchief in her hands tightly.

As Shadrach made his way through the wooded area, he approached a clear space. As he looked through the trees, he noticed all Slaves from the Plantation gathered around the pond with one another, holding hands and singing spirituals that were led by Big Debra. Tears filled his eyes as he watched his people sing and pray for better days.

Annabelle, who sat next to Eliza looked out into the wooded area; thinking that she may have seen a moving figure. As she looked harder into the area, she observed that her thoughts were correct; it was Shadrach hiding behind the trees, watching them pray. Although their eyes met, Annabelle did not say a word to anyone. She continued to sing and pray as if he were not there.

Shadrach sat down on the ground for a moment and re-thought his actions. Even though this journey to the North would be dangerous; he was determined to make it there as he did before. He began to cry for his people. In his heart he desired to save them all from bondage, but deep down he realized that it wasn't possible, for many of them were like Ola; they were adjusted to a Slavery mindset. A person had to first be able to invision a better life, before they could obtain one, and Shadrach new that.

He pulled himself together and moved forward, following the North Star. He felt more strong and powerful than ever. As he began running fast as he could through the woods, he held on to Ola's voice and his words of encouragement: "Never stop fighting, never stop believing." Those were the words that would lead him back to his freedom. He was determined to make his people proud.

Early the next morning, Annabelle awakened from the sunshine peeping through the cabin windows. She looked across the room at Gladdia sweating, coughing, and looking sickly than before. Annabelle rose from the bed. She wet a rag in a bowl of water and placed it on Gladdia's forehead,

"Mama hows ya feelin?....ya looks mighty bad mama, should I go git Big Debra to bring ova more herbs for ya?"

"I's be jus fine chile."

Gaddia replied,

"But I needs ya to work fo' me again today...tell the mistress I's be real sickly."

Annabelle looked at her mother and started to worry, but she showed no signs. She understood that she had to be strong for her during her time of hardship. There was no time for worrying. This was her time to prove to Daniel and Maryrose that inspite of her walking condition, she was well capable of pulling the weight for Gladdia and herself. She kissed her mother on the cheek, fed her the last of the herbs and set out for work.

As she walked through the Quarters, she met up with Big Debra, Eliza, and Noah, (Big Debra's other son). She smiled and greeted them all warmly.

"So did Gladdie make it to the main house fo work chile?"

asked Big Debra,

"Naw, she still in bed."

replied Annabelle,

"Still feelin sickly…and not lookin to good either."

Although Annabelle tried to hide her signs of worrying, Big Debra noticed them right away. She wrapped her big flabby arms around her and pulled her close to comfort her,

"No need in worrying chile."

she said,

"Lata on I runs ova to git my herbs and see bout her…she be jus fine in a few days.. my herbs neva lemme down!....you see."

Big Debra was like a second mother to Annabelle; she was mid-wife to her and always treated her kindly. She felt comfort in knowing that Gladdia would get better simply because Big Debra said that she would. That was enough comfirmation for her.
As they went there separate ways, Big Debra and Noah waved good-bye to them,

"See ya'll lata on!"

yelled Eliza. As the two of them walked through the field, Annabelle wondered to herself how

would she explain to Maryrose that Gladdia wasn't
coming to work. Eliza noticed the worried
expression on her face and grabbed her by the
hand,

"don't worry gal!....tween mama and her herbs, I
reckon Gladdie be good as new in a few days,
although I know she not be in a hurry to git back to
that ole place!"

they both smiled.

Annabelle and Eliza approached the Plantation
house and stood in front of the porch. Maryrose
walked out the front door toward the edge of the
porch and looked down at the both of them. Jimmy
followed behind her; his uniform jacket was
"inside out". Annabelle and Eliza noticed Jimmy's
jacket and giggled to themselves.
"And jus why do you two have dat strange grin on
yo faces!"

Maryrose asked,

"And where on earth is Gladdie…she due here by
now!"

Annabelle quickly removed the silly grin from her
face and grabbed Eliza's hand,

"She sick ma'am."

she replied,

"Big Debra an I been givn her herbs to git her betta….should be bak in a few mo' days."

"We takes care of the work load."

said Eliza,

"Wont be too hard to keep up,"

Annabelle released Eliza's hand and spoke proudly,

"Not be hard at all Mistress."

she said,

"Gits it all done by sunset, we's be more than able ma'am."

Annabelle and Eliza looked over at Jimmy; he was completely unaware that his suit jacket was being worn on the wrong side. They giggled more. Maryrose noticed his jacket and became nervous and frustrated. She spoke to Annabelle and Eliza in a sassy tone to remove the attention from Jimmy's jacket,

"Well then proud niggers…..git on in there and git to work!"

Annabelle and Eliza walked up the porch steps. They continued to stare at Jimmy and giggle quietly.

As they entered the house, Maryrose followed behind them. Before she walked through the front door, she looked over at Jimmy standing there; he was still unaware of his jacket being worn on the wrong side. Maryrose whispered to him in a demanding tone,

"JIMMY!...FIX YOUR JACKET FOR HEAVENS SAKE!"

Jimmy looked down at himself and noticed his jacket was on the wrong side. He became embarrassed and nervous. Jimmy did not want anyone to find out about him and Maryrose's secret affair. He took off his jacket and positioned it on the right side. He remained outside as Maryrose entered the house.

He stood out on the porch, looking out into the yard. He glanced his eyes toward heaven with tears in his eyes and spoke to God,

"The Mistress be wrong for what she make me do wit her, but I has no otha choice in the matta.....not wanna do it, but she make me. What's a man to do when he wants to do the right thing, but his life wont allow him too....what's a man to do lawd?"

As Jimmy stood out on the porch talking to God he knew that his situation with Maryrose would only get worst. They wouldn't be able to sneak around sleeping with each other without someone finding out.

VII

It was a beautiful day down at the Richmond Plantation. Jamison had been living there for over four years training under the leadership of Jackson Richmond. Jamison was in-charge of supervising the Slaves down in the Quarters and making sure that enough cotton was produced. He could be found in the cotton fields daily, pacing back and forth in his tailor made suit watching the Slaves work hard.

He often felt bad for them, being forced to work all day. Sometimes they would be punished and forced to work without a desent meal. Although Jamison did not like it, Jackson trained him to treat all Slaves this way. He said it taught them humility and how to be more grateful. Jamison disagreed with these tactics, yet it was his belief that he had to show respect by honoring Jackson's laws on the Plantation.

Jamison was considered to become main overseer of the Williamsburgh Plantation in another year, however; he did not intend to apply these same principles. He was older now, and he remembered his home and why his parents sent him away. His uncle McAuthor's spiritual lessons; and the love he had for Annabelle kept him strong throughout the years of being away from Williamsburg.

Jackson's attempt was to change Jamison's way of thinking, but he became stronger in his beliefs, but due to the cruelty shown in Southern States toward people who were against Slavery, Jamison was forced to keep his feelings to himself; and so he did.

One day, as Jamison stood in the cotton fields following his daily routine, he was approached by Jackson,

"I'm proud of how ya keepin the Slaves in line round here boy."
he said,

Jamison stopped and looked around the Plantation at each and every Slave. They were working so hard and diligently until you would think that they were earning a wage.

"Doesn't take much round here."

replied Jamison,

"They're pretty well structured."

Jackson looked out among the Slaves, and at the large acres that were overflowing with crop and cotton,

"Well as you know at Richmind, we have a very firm hand."

he said proudly,

"You've done a fine job here Jamison, I'm sure you will make ya people proud back at Williamsburg!.....and that Sophie of yours, I'm sure her and Maryrose will get along just fine."

Jamison thanked Jackson for his words of encouragement and shortly thereafter, the two of them departed ways. Before he could enjoy his moment alone to gather his thoughts accordingly, he was approached by his Fiance: Miss Sophie Clareheart of the Birmingham Clarehearts'.

"You've been out here too long wit these Slaves."

she said,

"Come now, I have cooked your favorite supper; chicken and gravy."

"Reminds me of my Gladdie's cooking back at the Plantation."

Jamison replied,

"And boy do I miss ma's homemade cherry pies"

Sophie walked closer to Jamison, clutching his arms tightly,
"Do you ever plan on tellin ya family bout us?"

she asked impatiently.

Sophie was madly inlove with Jamison. She was also infactuated with the fact that he was soon to become the main overseer of his Plantation. She preferred a man who had great amounts of power and influence.

"In due time Sophie…in due time."

he replied.

Jamison had no intentions on ever marrying Sophie. Although they were engaged, he only made that decision to hide the fact that he was inlove with Annabelle. It was her that he planned on moving away with to Canada, and even marrying one day.

Jamison kissed Sophie on the cheek.

"Why don't'cha run along and set the table for lunch dear."

he said,

Although Sophie obeyed his gesture, she went away wondering to herself if Jamison indeed loved her like he said, and if so; why wouldn't he mentioned her to his family in any of his letters. Why was he being so secretive about there engagement?

There was only one way to find out this information, and that was through his mother Maryrose. Sophie made up in her mind that maybe it was time to give Williamsburg Plantation a visit of her own. She wanted to find out for herself if there was a legitiment reason for Jamison keeping her a secret from his family; but not before confronted him one last time. She decided to ask once again after lunch; this time demanding a better response from him.

Thus after a long evening of eating and conversation with Jamison, Jackson, and his wife Elnora; Sophie respectfully asked to have a word with Jamison in the living room. As the two of them excused themselves and were alone; Sophie lashed out at him like an impatient spoiled little rich girl.
"Why would you propose to me and keep me a secret to your family?"

she asked,

Jamison remained silent for a moment. He took a deep breath, then began to express his feelings toward Sophie,

"Sophie you are a beautiful young lady. And let us not forget, it was
YOU who proposed to ME darling."

he replied,

"Same difference!"

said Sophie,

"Well these past four years have been remarkable, but I should've never accepted."

he said regretfully,

"Why not?"

Sophie asked,

"The proper thing to do when two people love one another is to git married!"

Jamison held his head down in shame for a moment, then looked her in the eyes,

"Although you're a great lady, there's someone else who has my heart Sophie, someone Ive known since I was a little boy, and until she sets me free; her love will hold me captive forever."

Sophie looked at him with disgust, then replied,

"So you accept my hand in marriage knowing that you had special feelings for someone else…..who is she Jamison? Is she back at Williamsburg waiting for you? Where did you meet her? Why hasn't she been here to see you?"

Jamison listened to Sophie's plea for an explanation and began feeling sorry for her. It was not his intentions to hurt her in any shape or form. He knew that if he were to speak the truth about Annabelle and who she really was, she would not have understood and would have caused more problems for him. Although he knew that eventually she would find out the truth, he decided to keep Annabelle's identity a secret for as long as he could.

"The love between me and her is complicated."

he said,

"I thought that if I tried real hard to give my heart to you, that it would help me forget about her…but the truth is Sophie, I don't want to forget about her."

Sophie's eyes filled with tears, she never imagined anyone coming along and taking her Jamison away from her.

"What's her name?"

Sophie asked?

"Who is this mystery lady that I should know about?"

Even though Jamison wanted to shout Annabelle's name from a mountain top and declare his love for her to the world, he chose to keep her name a secret.

"Think it's best that we change the subject."

he said.

"Don't want to upset you any more than I already have."

Sophie listened to Jamison' s explanation, then began having thoughts in her head that suggested maybe she should rely on Maryrose to give her the answers concerning this secret love affair. She looked Jamison in his eyes, the emotions that were building on her heart made it difficult for her to speak,

"I ....I have put too much into this relationship to lose you to some childish love affair that you had as a little boy!....I am willing to stand for my relationship! You were meant to be my husband, and I will not rest until it happens! So you tell your little friend back at Williamsburg that she may as well prepare for a battle....SOPHIE CLAREHEART IS NOT GOIN ANYWHERE!"

Sophie then turned away and swiftly walked away from the living room; leaving him there to ponder on his thoughts and her declaration. As he stood there thinking about the conversation that had transpired between the both of them, he began to think about Annabelle and the memory's he had of her back at the Plantation. It was only a matter of time before he would be back in her presence again; his only fear was that she would not remember him or the love they once shared with each other. He missed her deeply.

After spending a few more moments in the living room collecting himself, Jamison was interrupted by Jackson calling from the din area,

"JAMISON!....JAMISON!...GIT HERE BOY!"

he said loudly.

Jamison quickly made his way into the room and found Jackson going into the closet where he kept his shot guns, he began loading one with bullets.

"What's the matta Jackson?"

asked Jamison,

"Why are you loading your shot gun?"

"Just got word that a male Slave from your Plantation was caught in the woods not far from here"

replied Jackson,
"Looked like he was tryin to head North....I'm
gonna take Sophie home and then head out to help
jus in case there were more runaways wit
em....you comin along wit me?"

Listening to Jackson speak so anxiously about
catching runaway Slaves caused Jamison's heart to
beat at a steady pace. He loved every Slave on
Williamsburg Plantation and the thought of one of
them being captured and possibly killed caused
him to worry and become nervous.

"Naw..I betta stay here."

he replied,

"Need someone to keep watch over the
Plantation....u go ahead!"

"Very well then!"

said Jackson,

" I spose it be best you stayed round here
anyway....case something happens..there's another
shot gun in the closet if ya need it!"

Jackson grabbed his gun, and headed out of the
front door, Sophie was already outside waiting for
him. As they rode off into the trails, Jamison

immediately said a prayer for the runaway Slave being hunted.

His heart ached at the thought of what Daniel would do to punish him. It was that moment when he realized that this life was not for him, and that God had a better plan. He knew that sooner or later a day would come when he would have to leave Alabama and follow behind his uncle McAuthor, but Annabelle would have to be by his side, there was no other option. He could not leave the South without her.

Meanwhile, back at Williamsburg, Ola and Annabelle were in the kitchen preparing dinner. They had spent hours in the house cleaning and preparing. Ola was not saying much of anything to Annabelle, which was unusual, this caused her to become a little concern,

"Ola, ya be's alright?"
she asked,

"Been here most of the day fixing dinner and ya barely say a word...something troubling ya?"

Ola stopped stirring in the pot on the stove and paused for a moment. Deep inside she was disturbed, mostly worried about Shadrach and his safety.

"Reckon I be's okay...good lawd take care of errythang I guess."

Annabelle could sense that Ola had something deep on her mind that was troubling her; she became more concerned. Annabelle looked at Ola as an older sister.

She rose up from the table where she was sitting and walked over to the sink near the stove,

"Mama use to always say that a close mouf neva git no feedin."

 said Annabelle,

" You can tell me ….jus as if mama was standin in dis very spot!"

Ola began to chuckle to herself as she reflected on past conversations that were held between her and Gladdia in the kitchen,

"Humph!...if ya mama be's here, she worry me half to death til' I tells her errythang!"

Ola replied; then they both began to giggle silently. Ola stirred in the pot more. She looked out of the kitchen window into the fields. She decided to break her silence and tell Annabelle what was bothering her,

"My Shadrach come home to me the otha night…. he came to take me back wit em up nawlf."

Once Annabelle heard the word "North", she became excited. It reminded her of the stories that Jamison would talk about when she was younger; most of all, it reminded her of being free. Without realizing, she yelled out with excitement,

"NAWLF?"

Ola quickly put her finger in front of her own lips to suggest silence to Annabelle,

"Shhhhh, keep ya voice down gal!"

Ola whispered sternly,

"Yes…the nawlf!"

Once Annabelle realized the importance of keeping her voice low, she began to whisper loud enough for only Ola to hear her,

"Well why ya not go's wit em'….why ya stay here in dis awful place?"

Ola just held her head down for a moment, she often wondered to herself the same question. She walked over to the kitchen table and sat down. Annabelle leaned against the sink awaiting her explanation,

"Not be able to do no running."

Ola said,

"Be's too old now Anna….too late! Ya' be's young gal….you don't understand."

Annabelle looked over at Ola with confusion, then walked over and started stirring the pot on the stove. Ola began chopping vegetables,

"Well first chance I git to head dere…..I's runnin for my life. No matta how ole I be's."

Annabelle replied,
All of a sudden, as the two of them were in the kitchen preparing dinner, the Plantation bell began to ring in the background. Eliza came running into the kitchen with a dust rag in her hand. Ola rose up from the table with a nervous look in her eyes. Annabelle leaned over and looked out the window to see if she could see anything strange.

"What dey ringin the bell for?"

asked Eliza.

"Massa do's dat when he wonts us all to gatha round in the yard….usually fo a beatin, hangin, or announcement."

Ola replied nervously as the three of them walked out the backdoor of the kitchen and headed toward the bell.
All of the Slaves on the Plantation began walking toward the bell from the fields. They were

all looking nervous, scared and confused. There was an older Slave ringing the bell, the whipping chamber was also in position; this was not a good sign.

As all of the Slaves from the Plantation made there way to the yard, they found Daniel standing there with a whip in his hand. They all stood there quietly. The old Slave stopped ringing the bell and Daniel began speaking to everyone.

"Aiight!...listen to me real good. Don't plan on sayin dis but one time! Some of ya round here done got beside yaself….all dis walkin round here thankin ya ought to be treated betta than I treats ya'……I think its ungrateful!....down right ungrateful for ya niggers to act this way! I feed ya!....letcha have church, warm clothes in the winter, hell mos of ya have more than one pair of shoes, and ya still got nerve to wanna try and run off to seek ya freedom!...well I tellya….ya' aint gone fine it…ya aint gone fine it ever!"

As the Slaves all stood there listening to Daniel, wondering who he was referring to, Ola grabbed on to Annabelle's hand and held her head down in shame. She knew that her Shadrach ran away twice, but it wasn't because he was ungrateful; it was because he knew that he wasn't put on this earth to be treated like an animal. As Daniel stood there with the whip in his hands speaking to the crowd, she became nervous. What did he know? Ola could only hope and pray that nothing bad would happen to her. She had lived on

the Plantation all of her life and never been
beatened for anything.
Daniel began speaking more to the crowd,

"Ya' aint gone find it here…ya' all belongs to
me!...and just so none of ya' tries to get no clever
ideas…..figure I show ya' what happens to wheel
footin' niggers who tries to run away from their
masters."

Daniel yelled out toward the storage shed,

"GONE HEAD AND BRING EM' OUT HERE!"

Two bounty hunters, along with Jackson
Richmond of the Richmond Plantation dragged a
Slave from the storage shed. He was limping on
one leg as if he had a bad injury. The Slave was
chained by hands and feet and his lip and eye
appeared to be badly bruised. As Ola, Annabelle
and Eliza stood there with the other Slaves; they
were all shocked with surprise. The closer he got
to the whipping chamber, the more they all
recognized that it was Shadrach.
Ola fell down on her knees crying and screaming
loudly,

"NOOOOOO!.......NOOOOOOO!......NOT MY
SHADRACH!.....NOOOOOO!"

As Ola was on her knees crying and begging
for mercy, Big Debra, along with other older
female Slaves surrounded her in comfort. Shadrach

looked over at her with shame as the bounty
hunters locked him into the whipping chamber.
The more Ola looked at Shadrach, the louder she
cried out. Daniel yelled out to Ola,

"HUSH UP!....HUSH UP I SAY!"

"Shoulda told ya boy to stay put round here
stead of tryin to run off....gots to make em'
understand a niggers place round here. Gotta learn
respect for his master."

Daniel looked over at Jackson and the bounty
hunters and nodded his head. They snatched away
Shadrach's shirt and throwed two buckets of water
on his back. Some of the Slaves began crying,
others just stared in disbelief. As Shadrach hung in
the whipping chamber crying with water dripping
down his back, he looked toward heaven and
began praying silently,
"Lawd!....save me from this suffering lawd!....save
my peoples here on dis Plantation, I gives my heart
to ya lawd. Forgive me of my sinful ways.....save
me lawd!....if I dies, keep me close in ya arms."

Just as Shadrach ended his prayer time with God,
Daniel walked over and stood behind Shadrach
and rared his whip back, Annabelle screamed with
pain and passion in her voice, for she had never
witnessed anything so cruel,

"NOOOOOOOOOOOOOO MASSA!"

cried Annabelle as Daniel began whipping Shadrach's wet back with the whip.

As Daniel hit Shadrach, he screamed out in agony between each lash, the louder he screamed, the more Slaves cried out for him. Ola could hardly be contained.

The whip sliced Shadrach's back opened like a sharp knife, re-opening the wounds that were there from once before. His back was covered with blood and opened flesh. The water on his back caused the pain to be more severe. Shadrach screams were so loud and strident until Gladdia was able to hear him down in the Quarters. She cried for him as she layed in bed, shivering and coughing from sickness.

After ten lashes to Shadrach's back, his eyes were half way opened and he could hardly breathe. As the bounty hunters un-chained him, he fell to the ground and layed on his face in front of Ola. He began crawling to her slowly, blood pouring from his back.

Ola broke away and ran toward him, she fell down on her knees, lifted his head and looked him in his eyes, she was reminded of the words she spoke to him on the night he left her,

"God put in you his spirit…he will make you stand strong again as he is! Mighty as he is! Powerful jus as he is! Never Stop Fighting! Never stop Belieiving!"

Ola sat herself down on the ground. She grabbed Shadrach and positioned him across her lap. She held him tightly in her arms and began rocking him back and forth with tears in her eyes. As Shadrach layed there in her arms, shivering, sweating, and short of breath, Ola looked toward heaven and began whispering these words to him,

"Never stop fighting, never stop believing......never stop fighting, never stop believing...... never stop fighting, never stop believing."

She held him in her arms and repeated those words over and over. Not just for him, but for herself also.

As the other Slaves sadly turned around and headed back to the fields to continue working, Annabelle stood there in the yard, staring down at Ola and Shadrach. As Ola continued to rock Shadrach in her arms and whisper those words of encouragement to him, Annabelle began repeating the same words under her breath,

"Never stop fighting, never stop believing....never stop fighting, never stop believing......never stop fighting, never stop believing."

Afterward she looked into Ola's eyes and saw sadness, pain and sorrow. It was in that moment when they both realized, Shadrach would never be the same again.

Later on that evening, Annabelle finished her chores at the Plantation house and headed straight home to check on her mother. As she walked through the doors of the cabin, she found Gladdia lying in bed looking sickly than ever. She was sweating and coughing. Annabelle leaned over the bed and kissed her on the forehead.

"Mama...how ya feelin mama?"

she asked,

Gladdia started coughing so hard until she could barely speak. She managed to speak a few words to her,

"Fine....be's jus fine...ought not to worry bout me chile, God will take care a errythang."

As Annabelle stood over the bed looking down at Gladdia fighting for her life, Big Debra walked in with a basket of her herbal medicines. She leaned over and spoke to Gladdia in a soft calm voice,

"Hows ya holdin up Gladdie?"

she asked.

Gladdia was too weak to answer, she just layed there in bed while Big Debra rubbed her special ointment on her neck and chest.

It began to thunder outside, As Annabelle stood there watching her mother. The pain became too much for her to handle. The rainfall and strong winds from outside delivered a cold spirit inside of the cabin, as if death was trying to make an unexpected visit.

Big Debra sensed the spirit of death enter the room. She began praying softly for Gladdia. Annabelle became so upset until she ran out the front door of the cabin into the storm. She ran fast through the Quarters in the pouring rain. The wind was blowing hard and thunder cracked the skies. Annabelle ran so fast until her crippled leg caused her to stumble and fall unto the muddy ground. She picked herself up and continued to run until she reached the church.

She walked in slowly, dripping wet with mud all over her dress. She walked toward the front of the church as the moon shined in on her from the side window. She kneeled down on her knees and began to pray and talk to God. She lifted her hands high and cried out,

"LAWD!..I COME TO YA NOW!....NO WHERE ELSE TO GO!...NO WHERE ELSE TO TURN LAWD!.....I COME ASKIN' YA TO PLEASE TAKE CARE OF MY MAMA!...MAKE HER WHOLE AGAIN.....HEAL HER WIT' YA POWER!..HEAL HER WIT' YA POWER LAWD!....GIVE HER STRENGTH TO FIGHT!...I COME TO YA' ASKIN FO' YA HELP!....I CRY OUT!....I CRY OUT LAWD!...."

Annabelle began crying, the thunder became louder, as if her and death were having an argument. The rain poured down harder upon the land. Annabelle began praying louder,

"HELP US TO BE STRONG!.....TEACH US HOW TO FIGHT!....SET US FREE!....SET US FREE FROM THIS HARDSHIP WE BE FACING EVERYDAY!....SET US FREE!....SET US FREEEEEEE! LAWD I CALL ON YA' FOR STRENGTH AND POWER!.....FREE US LAWD!....FREEEE US!"

As Annabelle sat on her knees crying out to God, she became emotional and began waving her hands hysterically toward heaven as a symbol of surrendering to his mighty power. She cried out even more,

"WONTS TO BE FREE LAWD!....WONTS TO BE FREEEE!..."

While she was crying out to God, Shadrach passed by the doorway of the church and looked in on her. He did not say anything; he just stood there for a moment allowing the rain to drench his entire body. He watched her as she waved her hands and prayed, then he walked away slowly. Annabelle spent the remainder of that night in the church praying for her mother and the people on the Plantation. It was her only hope.

Annabelle woke up the next morning on the cold floors of the church. Her first thought was to go home and check on Gladdia. As she ran to the cabin as fast as she could, she found Gladdia sound asleep when she arrived.

Annabelle washed up and prepared herself for work. Eliza arrived shortly thereafter. The two of them began walking to Ola's cabin to meet up with her. As they approached the cabin, they found Shadrach sitting on the porch in an old chair with a blank stare on his face. As they got closer, Annabelle tried speaking to him,

"Howdy-doo Shadrach, how ya feelin dis' morning."

Shadrach didn't respond to her, he just continued to sit in the chair with a blank stare on his face. Annabelle and Eliza looked at each other with confusion. Shadrach had always been the type of man who was extremely friendly and fluent in conversation,

"Reckon you can tell Ola we's out here waitin fo her?"

Eliza asked him,

Annabelle looked toward the cabin door and yelled for Ola until she came out. Shadrach continued to sit on the porch; not saying a mumbling word.

"Ya don't have to yell so loud!"

Ola shouted,

"I's comin…ya' know I gits right excited to go workin fo the good ole massa….jus loves how he works me half to death!"

Annabelle and Eliza didn't say anything, they just giggle to themselves at the sarcastic remark. Before they left, Ola leaned over and kissed Shadrach on the cheek; he continued to sit with a blank stare on his face and no response. Annabelle and Eliza held there head down to show respect as Ola walked down the cabin steps to join them. As the three of them walked together toward the Plantation house, Eliza decided to ask Ola about Shadrach,

"What be's the matta wit Shadrach?"

she asked,

"Why he not say nothin?"

Annabelle nudged Eliza on the arm,

"You neva mind that gal!"

said Annabelle,

"Ola ya not has to speak on it if ya' don't want too."

Ola and the girls were silent for a moment with only the sounds of their feet trailing through the grass; finally, after about five minutes of silence; Ola decided to explain,

"Seem like when dey beats my Shadrach, dey beat the life right out of em…..he not say two words to me since dat day. He wake up sometime in the middle of the night cryin'…I not know what to do for em cept pray. My mind tells me his body be's here wit me…but his heart be still up nawlf where he was free!.....I feels like it all be my fault…..cause of me, my Shadrach loss his soul!"

As Ola continued talking to Annabelle and Eliza, a tear rolled down her cheek. No one said anything else. Annabelle and Eliza felt sorry for her. They grabbed Ola by the hand and continued to walk toward the Plantation house for work. As they approached the house, they noticed Jimmy and Maryrose walking toward the storage shed, they stared in disbelief for a brief moment.

"Best look straight ahead and keep a walkin!"

 said Ola sternly,

"Dat woman be doin' somethin shameful before the lawd….po' Jimmy….. he caught up in a bad place."

As they all got closer to the house, Annabelle was reminded of apples that she was instructed to gather for pies.

"My…I almost forgot!"

she cried out,

"I promised the mistress that I would go out dis morning and bring in a basket of apples for pies later"

said Annabelle,

"Y'all go on in the house!"

"You plan to walk way out there to them apple trees by yaself?"

asked Eliza,

"Dats way out passed the Quarters!"

Annabelle took a deep sigh; partly from frustration and the rest from irritation.

"Has no otha choice, less ya comin wit me"

she replied,

"I has to get started on the floors"

cried Eliza,

"Well I has no otha choice but to do it alone."

said Annabelle,

She walked over to the side of the house and picked up a basket; then headed out into the fields to collect the apples that Maryrose requested of her. Ola and Eliza went inside and prepared for work.

As Annabelle made her way through the fields carrying her empty basket, she couldn't help but reflect back on the memories of her and Jamison. She imagined them playing around and talking in there favorite spot under the fig tree. She walked pass the sugarcane and cotton fields and wondered to herself if she would ever see a new life, a life that would allow her to be free from bondage. Would Jamison ever come back to Williamsburg, and if he did; would he remember her and the special times they shared.

Annabelle tried to erase the memories of him from her mind but had difficulty; yet after a dreadful walk through the fields, daydreaming and reminiscing, she approached her destination. There was a great deal of apples that had fallen to the ground. She decided to graze through a few of them, checking to see if they were fresh enough to put in her basket. As she began filling her basket with only the best apples that she could retrieve, she over heard the sound of horses in the background; all of a sudden, she found herself surrounded by three white men. She dropped her basket of apples to the ground and stood still, preparing herself for anything at that moment. The three men didn't say anything accept for

"GRAB HER!"

Instantly they jumped down from there horses and put a potato bag over her head. Annabelle's first reaction was to scream but she did not want them to kill her. She remained as silent as possible and cooperated with there commands. They threw her on one of the horses and rode off into the wooded area; no one noticed anything.

As Annabelle rode on the back of the horse, listening for any background noises to give her a clue as to where they were taking her; she prayed silently for protection. After minutes of riding through the woods, they finally came to an abandoned barn. The men snatched her from the horse and threw her unto the ground. Annabelle removed the potato bag from over her head and layed there crying and begging them for mercy. She looked up at them with fear in her eyes. Suddenly, they began ripping her dress from her until she was completely naked.

"Stoppit please!....why are you doin dis!"

 she cried out as she layed on the ground naked and ashamed. The men took off their clothes and forced themselves on her. Annabelle layed there and cried as they each took there time beating and sexually abusing her one after the other. Each one of them would roughly force their erected penis inside of her and thrust hard, as if they were intentionally trying to hurt her.

They strangled her until she was almost out of breath and bit on the nipples of her breasts until they were almost bleeding. Mentally, she could not understand why this was happening. Who were these men and why were they doing this to her? Annabelle just layed there on her stomach and prayed for the cruelty to end. Each minute was as if it lasted for hours.

As she layed there on the ground, she looked forward and noticed a woman peeping in from a doorway. Who was this woman and how could she stand there and watch these men abuse her? Annabelle had no idea that this woman was Sophie Clareheart, Jamison's fiancé.

After learning more about Annabelle through Maryrose, they secretly arranged for these men to physically hurt her. They both agreed that if she survived, they could at least ruin her female organs so that Jamison would no longer have an interest in her when he returned to Williamsburg. She would no longer be considered fresh and she would become unattractive to him.

Sophie stood in the doorway of the abandoned barn, watching these men do those awful things to Annabelle without feeling any sympathy or compassion. They handled her so roughly until she began bleeding from her anal and vaginal areas. After almost an hour of this cruelty, when Annabelle was at the point of almost losing consciousness, Sophie and the three men left her there in hopes that she would bleed to death and die; but God had another plan.

Annabelle layed on the ground for almost thirty minutes, barely able to move, she could feel the warm blood running down her legs. Although she barely had enough energy, she possessed a strong determination and eagerness to live. She layed there for a moment and prayed to God, asking him to give her strength and courage to get up from the ground. After a few minutes of praying, she was able to maintain herself.

With only a plow wood stick to aid her in walking, Annabelle managed to make it out of the barn and onto the trail leading through the woods. Annabelle walked and walked slowly on the trail for an hour. A man from a nearby Plantation came riding by in a covered wagon; he noticed her in the distance and slowed down,

"Where ya goin wit all dat blood on ya gal….ya been hurt?"

he asked as he looked at her strangely,

"Be's from Williamsburg Plantation massa."

Annabelle replied,

"I's be hurtin mighty bad…..please help me git dere suh."

The man looked down at her and noticed the Plantation tags around her neck,

"Well come on and git in!"

he said,

 "No need in gettn yoself in mo' trouble out here in these woods…. A dead nigga can't be much use to its massa ..and you looks half dead gal!"

He helped Annabelle climb aboard the wagon. She thanked him repeatedly as he drove her back to Williamsburg. She kindly directed him to drop her off under the apple trees where she was kidnapped originally. She was too ashamed to allow anyone to see her in that condition. The driver did as she asked and drove away swiftly. The abuse and injuries weakened her so intensely until she became dizzy and fainted under the apple tree.

Back at the Plantation house, Eliza and Ola were busy in the kitchen, preparing things for lunch and supper. Ola sat at the table shelling peas and daydreaming as Eliza pranced back and forth doing little things to make there work load easier. She walked into the pantry and found a full barrel of apples.

"Don't know why the mistress would send Annabelle for apples dis moanin, we has plenty right here!"

she said.

Ola didnt reply to Eliza's remarks, instead she continued to shell peas and daydream. Eliza walked closer to Ola and sat down at the kitchen table,

"Didya hear me Ola?.....I said there's a full barrel of apples in that there pantry!"

Ola stopped shelling peas and looked over at Eliza,

"I heard ya' the first time chile, jus' sittin here thinkin bout my Shadrach."

she replied,

"Wish he would least tell me what's troubling him.....know if massa did to me what he did to him, I wouldn't have much to say either I reckon."

Eliza reached across the table and grabbed Ola's hand,

"Ya has to give him a chance to come around Ola."
she said,

"When the massa beat him half to death like he did, I think apart of his soul left out of em and left him hopeless......maybe ya' has to pray it back."

Ola stood up from the kitchen table and walked toward the kitchen sink, she looked out the window into the yard. Tears built in her eyes as she began to speak softly,

"None of dis wouldn't be goin on wit my Shadrach if I would have jus went wit em when he ask me too......now my Shadrach may neva speak to me again!"

After Ola spoke those words, she held her head down and cried at the sink. Eliza quickly ran over to comfort her. She put her hands on her shoulders and began to rub them gently,

"Ya can't blame yaself for what happened to Shadrach Ola, ya has to be strong and help em git through this hard time he be facing.....ya all he got right nah Ola, he needs ya."

Ola listend to Eliza, wiped her eyes with the corner of her dress and looked her straight in the eyes without blinking,

"Who's gonna take care of me Liza!"

she asked,

"Who's gonna take care of me?"

As Ola began to cry harder, Eliza grabbed Ola by the hands and said to her softly,

"Same person who's been takin' care all of us on dis here plantation.....God almighty!"

Eliza walked back over to the kitchen table and sat down to finish shelling the peas. Ola continued to stand at the sink,

"Liza, you becoming more and more like ya mama as the days go on, ya gonna be as strong as she is."

Ola said,

"Anna always tell me that once we become older, we will have to be strong enough to fight the hardships on dis here Plantation, so us may as well start right nah!"

replied Eliza,

"And where is Anna?.....shoulda been back by now with those EXTRA apples the mistress sends her after."

Eliza stood from the table, she and Ola both looked out the kitchen window into the yard to see if there was any sign of Annabelle walking through the fields,

"Wonder what's takin' her so long?"

Ola said,

"Maybe you oughta go out to the apple trees and see what's keepin' her chile."

Eliza didn't make a response, she just walked toward the back door of the kitchen and headed out into the fields, Ola watched from the window.

Eliza walked through the fields swiftly, praying to God that everything was okay with Annabelle. Although the apple trees were only a few feet away from the fields, the blazing sun made the walk seem longer than normal. As she walked pass the cotton and sugarcane fields, she could see the apple trees in the distance. The closer she approached the trees, the more nervous she became. Where was Annabelle?

As she approached the apple trees, she looked around the area; calling Annabelle's name loudly. There was no answer. She began walking around the trees, looking for any signs or clues. She looked closer and harder, suddenly she noticed Annabelle's leg from the corner of one of the trees. Eliza screamed with terror and ran over to where Annabelle was laying helplessly with blood all over her lower body. She kneeled down to see if she was alive. She was barely breathing.

Eliza shook her continuously trying to revive her, but nothing happened. She began to cry, she thought that her bestfriend was dieing. Eliza stood up and screamed loud for help. She began running and waving her hands in the air. She ran toward the sugarcane fields where Big Debra was working. Eliza screamed louder and waved her hands more wildly. The closer she got to the fields, the more the other Slaves heard her.

"HELP!....HELP ME PLEASE!......MAMA!... SOMETHING HAS HAPPENED TO ANNA!.....COME QUICK... BY THE APPLE TREES."

Everyone stopped what they were doing and ran over to Eliza,

"Whats the matta chile?"

asked Big Debra frantically,

"It's Anna!"

cried Eliza,

"She's laying out by the apple trees, there's blood all over her!....something has happened to her!"

   Big Debra and Eliza ran over to the cotton fields to inform Noah and the three of them ran to the apple trees to save Annabelle. When they arrived, Big Debra looked down at her; she saw the blood and torn dress. She immediately knew what happened.

 "Oh my God!...who done dis to you chile!"

she cried out.

"Noah!...grab her legs…Liza, you help me with her arms…..we gone take her back to my cabin…..can't let Gladdie see her like dis!"

Big Debra said.

Noah grabbed both of Annabelle's legs, Big Debra and Eliza grabbed her arms. They carried her through the Quarters to the cabin to be cleaned up and nursed back to health. Once they arrived, they gently placed Annabelle on the bed. Big Debra used a homemade strong aroma under her nose to awake her. Once she regained consciouness, she began to cry uncontrollably,

"They tried to kill me.....they tried to kill me!"

 she cried out as Big Debra and Eliza focused on trying to keep her calm.

"Just calm down Anna....calm down."

Big Debra said softly while cleaning her up.

 "I got something imma put on ya down dere....will heal ya up jus fine chile, may sting ya a little."

Eliza and Noah stood back and watched as Big Debra cleaned all the blood from Annabelle with a soft rag. Eliza's eyes were filled with tears, it hurted to see her bestfriend in so much pain.

 "I's gotta git back to the Plantation house."

she said,

"The mistress be lookin for Anna soon, I gots to let her know what happened."

Big Debra reached over and grabbed a bowl of homemade ointment that she made from natural herbs.

"First I needya to come over and hold Anna's hand."

she said,

Eliza walked over and obeyed her mother's command. She rubbed Annabelle's hands gently and assured her that everything would be okay. Big Debra began rubbing ointment on Annabelle's private parts. The ointment caused a burning sensation on her tender areas, causing her to cry out loudly,

"Has to put this on ya!"

said Big Debra,

" If ya ever wanna heal right to bare chilrens."

Annabelle cried and cried, not from the ointment; but from the hurt and shame she was feeling. Noah stood there in disbelief. The situation became so unbearable until he left the room and sat on the porch.

"Alright now chile, you got to tell us what happened to ya."

Annabelle remained silent for a moment. She did not want to remember, yet after a few minutes of nothing but crying, she decided to break her silence. Tears fell slowly from their eyes as Annabelle told the story of what happened to her in the woods. She begged Eliza and Big Debra to not mention it to anyone, and insisted that she return with Eliza to the Plantation house for work.

Annabelle was in pain from her attack, however; she felt that going back to work would be the best decision. Maryrose had previously given her a hard time concerning Gladdia's work load, thus she did not want to make matters worst. After cleaning thoroughly and applying more ointment, she was able to change her dress and head back to work with Eliza as if nothing ever happened. Noah returned to the fields. He made a declaration to God and Annabelle that he would not mention to anyone what he witnessed in that hour. Masses of hidden secrets were known to dwell in the Williamsburg home; however, the Slave cabins were known to carry mysteries untold. The Slaves were strong enough to endure pain beyond anyone's imagination. They had no other choice.

VIII

Annabelle, Eliza, and Ola were busy working in the kitchen. Eliza was washing the dishes, Ola was mixing cake batter in a bowl and Annabelle was mopping the wooden floors. They were quietly sharing a conversation with each other when suddenly Maryrose came prancing in the room eating a pickle. She walked toward the kitchen window,

"Oh, isn't it a beautiful day for a picnic in the yard?"

she asked,

"Think I'd like to have this years social outside….I know a great deal of people now then last year!...the girls will all be delighted!"

Maryrose turned from the window and glanced over at Annabelle struggling to clean a stubborn stain on the floor. Considering the cruel plan she made with Sophie Clareheart, she was utterly surprised to find Annabelle working with the others.

"Anna, ya think Gladdie be well enough to do some cookin for the social?"

Annabelle stopped mopping for a second and took a deep pause. The fact that Maryrose was only concerned about having her best cook available bothered her deeply. Although she was hoping for the best, she was not looking forward to seeing her mother being taken advantage of again. Inspite of her feelings concerning this matter, she looked up at Maryrose and responded pleasantly with a smile,

"God willin Mistress.....God willin."

"Well I needya girls to hurry and prepare dinner."

Maryrose said anxiously,

"Think ima have Miss Ruth over for dinner to help me plan the social.......now chop! chop!"

After giving her commands, Maryrose left the others to attend to their duties.

"For long, the Mistress gone have mo' to worry bout than dat social of hers she be planning."

said Annabelle as she continued to mop the floors.

Eliza stopped washing dishes and sat down at the kitchen table. She whispered so only Ola and Annabelle would hear,

"Saw my brotha Jimmy walkin out dat shed wit her two and three times a week for the past few months….I's not say nothing to mama bout it, although I figure she already know."

Ola looked at Annabelle and Eliza with a serious look in her eyes. She knew about the secret affair between Jimmy and Maryrose, yet she did not entertain the gossip. She gave a word of advice to them both,

"Best mind what ya say round here…..good lawd take care a errythang! If the massa would stay out the Quarters most of the time….then the Mistress wont have to go fetching for Jimmy like she do!...........most time I wish God would jus close dese ole eyes a mine, be's betta off not seein what go on round here!"

Annabelle and Eliza became silent for a moment, then continued on with there work,

"Reckon there gone be a lot of peoples here at the social?"

Annabelle asked,
"Member laz time the house was full of folk from everywhere!"

"Spose there will be."

replied Ola,

"The Mistress has us all round here doin all the cookin and cleanin and she git all the glory!......humph! all dat white woman been doin the past few weeks is stuffing herself with food, apple pies, and PICKLES!"

They all laughed at the thought of Maryrose doing anything other than talking and eating. Work for her was un-heard of.

After an hour of cooking and preparing supper, Annabelle and Eliza decided to go out and pull sheets from the clothes line. They had been sharing there thoughts and secrets with one another since they were little girls. Pulling sheets was an opportunity to have a private conversation without involving the others. They looked forward to spending time with each other there.

Ola would peep out from the kitchen window from time to time to ensure that they were working diligently. Maryrose had a low tolerance for servants who slacked on there duties, she would have them beatened with no hesitation, especially Gladdia, nevertheless; as Annabelle and Eliza carefully took down the sheets, they began to share a conversation,

"Jus can't help but thank bout what massa did to Shadrach....not right what he did."

said Annabelle,

"Errytime dat whip hit across his back, my heart jump!.....now massa done took away his voice….and his pride right long wit it!"

Eliza pulled a sheet down from the line, Annabelle grabbed the opposite end and they folded it together neatly, making sure that all ends were lined evenly,

"Feels bad for Ola."

replied Eliza,

"Reckon it take a lot outta her to see the man she love git beat half to death…den sent back to the fields to die!.....humph! mama say: us born in the fields…..us die in the fields!"

Annabelle positioned the sheet in the basket, then grabbed Eliza by the arm,

"We's not dieing no where on dis Plantation!"

she said,

"We's gonna run off to the nawlf and marry us well to do gentleman."

Annabelle began strutting around the yard proudly, then continued on with her fairy-tale story,

"Us gone live in big houses wit apple trees, gardens and flowers…I'm gonna take errybody wit me who wants to come along!"

Eliza smiled as she listened to Annabelle boast about her dreams of becoming a free woman, then she asked Annabelle a serious question,

"How ya ma' doin?....she gettn any betta?"

Eliza folded the last sheet from the line and awaited an answer. Annabelle was aware of her mother's situation, and it wasn't getting any better; but rather than tell Eliza the truth, she remained silent, holding back her tears. Eliza saw the pain on Annabelle's face. She walked over and grabbed her by the hand to comfort her,

"You can tell me the truth Anna, is she gonna be okay?"

Annabelle stood in the middle of the yard; tears began building in her eyes. The thought of her mother being sick caused her to worry, but nevertheless; she had faith that she would recover soon.

"Come wit me to the Quarters."
Annabelle replied,

"I let you see fo yaself jus how she be doin."

"Well what bout supper?"

asked Eliza,

"Supper be just about done and Ola can finish up the rest!"

replied Annabelle,

"Now c'mon!.....ma' be's happy to see you!"

Ola looked out the kitchen window at the two of them; she watched as they grabbed each other by the hand and made their way toward the Quarters.

While they were walking, Annabelle began praying silently, it was one of the things that she learned when she was a little girl, to pray whenever times got hard. Eliza over-heard her and began praying as well. As the two of them were walking, they both hoped for the best when they arrived. Although they were aware of Gladdia's condition, it would hurt them deeply to find that things had gotten worse. They slowed down their stride for a moment, hoping to prolong the journey. Annabelle mentioned different subjects along the way to ease the moment and take their minds off of Gladdia's situation.

"I spose Shadrach shoulda took Ola along wit em' the first time he left."

said Annabelle,

"Dat way he neva woulda had to come back in the first place!....down right foolish it was!"

Eliza looked over at Annabelle with a slight smirk on her face, pondering if she should respond to her comment about Shadrach; it was only seconds later when she decided to go ahead and reply,
"Well gal you talks bout leavin here headed nawlf wit half the Slaves and a WHITE BOY!...... dat sounds mo' foolish to me than anything else!"

Annabelle stopped walking for a moment and looked over at Eliza. Even though her comments were somewhat true, she was shocked to hear them come from her.

"Aint said nothing bout leavin here wit no WHITE BOY!"

she said,

"He been gone away so long....maybe he not even know who I am when he come back....dats IF HE EVEN COME BACK!"

Annabelle paused for a moment, then continued explaining,

"When I decide to leave dis place, it be's on my own.....me and God....think I may bring you along too Liza!....you be's my best friend and all."

Eliza looked over at Annabelle; her facial expressions suggested that she was slightly confused,

"Sho hope you has a better plan than ole Shadrach did!"
she replied,

"Or we's be in a heap a trouble sho nuff!"

They both began laughing and shrugging each other teasingly. They stopped for a moment and looked ahead. Among the trees were the Quarters and Annabelle's cabin.
Both of their hearts began to beat rapidly, fear sat in their minds and nervousness caused them to tremble. Eliza grabbed Annabelle by the hand, not a word was said. They both looked straight ahead and walked forward. They reached the steps of the cabin and stood there staring at the door, suddenly; the door swung openly swiftly with Big Debra walking from it; scared Annabelle and Eliza speechless.

"Heavens sake!....like to have scared you both half to death!"
said Big Debra,

"I was jus comin to look fo ya Anna, ya best come on in here."

Annabelle and Eliza both look at each other, they took a deep breathe and walked up the cabin steps into the room. They walked in and stood on the side of the bed where Gladdia was laying. She appeared to be weak, sweating and coughing.

"Sound pretty bad…why ya herbs not help her git betta Big Debra?"

 asked Annabelle,

Big Debra looked over at Annabelle standing beside Eliza holding her hand. The look on her face caused them both to worry even more. She pulled them over to the corner of the room and whispered,

"Malaria….she got Malaria….not much I can do any mo chile….only try to make it easy fo her".

Annabelle tried with all of her might to keep her emotions under control, but looking over at her mother struggling for her life caused her to become upset. She ran over to the bed-side and fell down on her knees. She cried for Gladdia. Big Debra and Eliza walked over slowly and put there hands on her back for comfort. They all looked worried.

"SHE CAN'T DIE!"

cried Annabelle,

"WHAT I'S GONE DO WITHOUT MY MAMA?"

Annabelle lifted her head and looked over at Gladdia,

"Mama!....can't leave me mama…I…I take good care of ya til ya git betta!....jus don't leave me mama!...ya hear me!.....do ya hears me mama!!!"

Annabelle layed her head beside Gladdia and cried harder.
Gladdia took her left hand and began lightly stroking Annabelle's hair, although she was coughing and short of breath, she forced herself to get these words out,

"Don't cry chile….dont cry for me….this here be the good lawds will for me….dis be his plan chile….I not fight wit em….I's let him have control over it all."

She then leaned over and embraced Annabelle's face,

"Ya be's a grown woman nah!"

she said in a light whisper,

"I knew the time would come when I would have to leave ya…..I jus thank the good lawd fo bein able to see how beautiful you become."

Gladdia then looked over at Big Debra standing behind Annabelle with Eliza, she reached her hand out to her; Big Debra then walked over and grabbed it gently,

"Don't let the massa hurt my baby."

Gladdia said,

"She be my sweet, sweet, baby."

Big Debra began to cry silently, she understood that Gladdia was preparing herself to die. Annabelle became very emotional, she began speaking and crying hysterically,

"MAMA!....KNOW ONE IS GONNA HURT ME....DONT TALK DAT WAY MAMA!....EVERYTHING WILL BE JUST FINE....YOU SEE!"

Gladdia turned away from them and looked toward the ceiling, as if she was looking toward heaven, she began to speak softly,

"You be's a strong gal Anna, since ya was a baby....always been strong....please don't let the massa hurt ya like he hurt me Anna.....don't let em do what he did to me. He tried......he tried to keep ya from lovin dat boy!......he tried to keep ya papi from lovin me.....dont let em ruin ya baby!"

Annabelle stood up from the floor and looked over the bed at Gladdia,

"Mama!....mama don't leave me mama!....I know what he did to ya..I remember it all, I remember it all mama and I will help ya be strong…jus hold on mama!....fight mama!....ya gots to fight!!"

Annabelle turned and looked to Big Debra for help,

"Big Debra!....tell mama to fight!......tell her we needs her!....tell her she cant leave us!"

she cried as she fell down on her knees and grabbed Gladdia's hand.

"I's tide Anna."

she said,

"I's be mighty tide….this here sickness done took ova my body….nothin I can do nah….but I not worry cause I know as long as I be in heaven….massa cant hurt me no mo….I jus want ya to do one thing baby….."

"ANYTHING!"

cried Annabelle,

"Anything fo ya mama!"

Gladdia stopped looking at the ceiling and looked over to Annabelle and grabbed her hand,

"Wontcha to forgive him baby."

she said,
"Forgive the massa fo hurtin us, only way you gone make it through life…..ya has to forgive people who hurt ya baby."

Annabelle just looked at Gladdia with tears pouring down her face and nodded her head forward,

"Yes!....yes mama!....I forgive him!"

Suddenly Gladdia turned and faced the opposite side of the room. She stared at the wall with tears slowly streaming from her eyes. She began to speak slow and clear, coughing between words;

"Got somethin to tell ya baby."

Gladdia said,

"When you were jus a baby, I come home to the cabin after workin in the house….ya papi, he was right troubled inside cause of the way massa had been mis-treatin me…..we yelled at each other all night long….I falls asleep shortly after and I….I woke up to a loud noise, massa had come down wit the bounty hunters and took ya papi way from here…I watch him lay you down in the cradle and go off wit em….when I woke up the next moanin…ya papi was still gone…..later on dat moanin we found him dead hangin from a tree….it was then I knew…..it was then I knew chile….the massa killed ya papi!.....he took him away from us baby… ya papi did not kill himself, the massa killed him."

Annabelle looked at Gladdia in disbelief and cried out,

"Noooo mama!...please don't let it be true….he took my papi away from me??…."

Gladdia felt herself become feeble; she could barely keep her eyes opened, she gained enough strength to utter these few little words to Annabelle,

"Must forgive him chile….must for-give him." After Gladdia spoke those words, she leaned her head over to the side, took her last breath, closed her eyes softly and died instantly. Annabelle began shaking her and crying out,

"MAMA!....MAMA PLEASE GIT UP!.....GIT UP MAMA!....MAMA!......MAMA! DON'T LEAVE ME MAMAAAAAA!"

She layed her head in Gladdia's lap and cried hysterically, Big Debra rubbed her back to comfort her. Eliza stood in the background praying and crying silently. Suddenly after a few more minutes of grieving, Annabelle lifted her head, rose up from Gladdia's bedside and ran as fast as she could out the front door. Eliza yelled out to her,

"NO ANNA!....COME BACK!....COME BACK ANNA!"

Eliza tried running after her but was stopped by Big Debra. She grabbed her by the arm and whispered these words,

"Let her go chile…..she be hurtin…jus let her go."

Annabelle ran through the Quarters with tears streaming down her face, her mind was filled with questions that remained un-answered. She was upset that her mother passed away and angry that Daniel killed her father. She thought about those men who abused her physically, sexually and mentally. With all of those emotions crowding inside of her head, she was forced to run toward the Plantation house. She ran so hard until her crippled leg began to ache and swell, she also began to feel soreness from her private areas; but she did not allow that to stop her. Annabelle was determined to confront the man that killed her father and abused her mother the way those men abused her.

The closer she moved toward the Plantation house, the more she forgot about her aching legs and soreness. The pain in her heart provided her with enough strength to run even faster. As she approached the house, she noticed a light coming from the storage shed; she ran in that direction instead. When Annabelle arrived to the shed, a female Slave walked out just as she was preparing to walk in. Annabelle stared at her strangely. The Slave said nothing, just held her head down in shame and walked toward the Quarters. Annabelle watched her walk away; wondering to herself, if he had done the same thing to her as he did to Gladdia. She entered the storage shed through the front door. When she walked in, she found Daniel sitting on a pile of hay finishing up a glass of Brandy. The sound of Annabelle breathing grabbed his attention, he turned around and noticed her standing there staring at him as if she wanted to kill him,

"What brings ya hear gal!"

he asked,

 "Shouldn't ya be down in the Quarters tendin to ya sick mama!"

    She walked closer to him with anger and tears in her eyes, hands trembling from nervousness; heart pounding from anxiety. She murmured under her breath loud enough for only him to understand,

 "My mama be's dead massa!....she be's dead and you's the one dat killed her!.....cause of you she had a broken heart and gave up on fighting!....she die cause of yo hate and evil ways!"

    Daniel heard the news from Annabelle and became upset. Although he treated Gladdia badly; he was secretly inlove with her. He stood from the haystack and tossed his glass to the side. He grabbed Annabelle firmly by the arms and began speaking to her loudly; almost yelling,

"DONTCHA BE COMIN HERE TELLING LIES GAL!"

he said,

"I'LL WHIP YA GOOD FOR LIEING TO ME!"

Annabelle looked Daniel in his eyes and spoke with certainty,

"She be DEAD suh!...she got tide a fighting and dies right in front of me, Liza and Big Debra." Daniel could feel tears building in his eyes from hurt and regret, he pushed Annabelle abruptly and walked to the other side of the shed; hiding his face from her,

"Well when did it happen...when did she pass?"

he asked.

"Not long afta I git dere from workin."

Annabelle replied,

"She tell me errythang...before she die, she tell me errythang you done to her and my papi!"

As Annabelle was speaking to Daniel, she suddenly felt confidence rise up on the inside of her, a spirit of boldness overtook her; she was no longer afraid of what Daniel may do to hurt her. She wanted to express her feelings and this was the only way. She walked over to where he stood, looked at him in his eyes and spoke loud with a clear tone,

"She tell me how ya hurt her!.....I remember watchin ya do thangs to her dat make her shame before God!!!....she tell me how ya cause trouble tween her and papi....how ya made him feel less than a man and how you TOOK HIS LIFE FROM HIM!!!!"

Daniel listened to Annabelle express her feelings until he could hardly handle them anymore; guilt began to confront him of his evil ways. Suddenly he reared back his hand and slapped her face so hard until she staggered and fell to the ground,

"ENOUGH!"

he said,

"I order you to go back to the Quarters NOW!! …and never speak of dis again…..you understand me GAL!!"
Annabelle layed there and stared at him with a mean look on her face; un-moved by his commands; with tears slowing streaming from her

eyes, she rose up from the ground and spoke these words to him,

"Ya kills my papi!"

Daniel became more frustrated and the confrontation made him angry, he put his right hand on her throat and slammed her againt the wall; he yelled louder at her; practically screaming,

"GAL…I SAID YOU RETURN BACK TO THE QUARTERS NOW!!!!!"
Annabelle snatched away from him and ran to the other side of the shed. Although she knew that she could be punished for disobeying Daniel, her heart would not be at peace until she confronted him completely. She began yelling to the top of her lungs,

"YOU KILLS MY MAMA AND MY PAPI AND I HOPE YOU
ROTT IN HELL!!!!!"

As she screamed at Daniel and released her anger, she instantly felt a heavy load lift from her shoulders, she felt light as a feather in that moment. Daniel looked over at her and walked over to where she was standing. He grabbed her by the arms, pulled her closer to him and began kissing her aggressively as if she were Gladdia.
Annabelle pulled away from Daniel and slapped him in the face, Daniel slapped her harder and she fell to the ground; nose dripping with

blood. When Annabelle fell, she noticed a piece of plow wood lieing on the ground beside her. She grabbed the wood, stood up quickly and hit Daniel hard across his face. He fell to the ground with his face and mouth full of blood. She looked down at him lying there unconscious. She dropped the wood on the ground and ran quickly from the storage shed.

As Annabelle ran through the fields crying from hurt, anger and fear; she was reminded of what Jamison told her about the pond years ago when they were only children. She thought about the men who abused her, her mother and father dieing and Daniel; who was sure to have her whipped once he regained consciousness. Annabelle only looked forward and ran toward the pond outside of the Quarters.

As she was running she began praying to God, asking him to protect and keep the hand of Daniel from killing her. She also prayed for her mother's soul and that Heaven would greet her with open arms. She prayed for the men who abused her in the abandoned barn, she also asked God to protect Jamison and bring him back home safely.
When Annabelle arrived at the pond, she stood there for a moment, breathing hard; body drenching from sweat. Her feet were sore and scraped from running bare footed. Her private areas were still sore from the abuse she suffered. She thought about what Jamison said to her years ago, how he spoke about people getting into the pond and allowing God to wash away their pain and heal them of their troubles.

Although she was skeptical, she instantly took off her dress and limped over closer to the pond. Her crippled leg caused her to trip and fall into the water. She stood up and began splashing and throwing water all over her body wildly until she was completely wet. As she washed her body with the water, she began praying to God,

"Clean me!....clean me lawd!.....wash away the pain....wash away the hurt!....come into my life lawd!.....clean me from all dis pain I feel....do ya hear me?....ya hear me lawd?"

Then she began praying louder and splashing more water on her body,

"CLEAN ME!.....CLEAN ME LAWD!.....WASH ME!......TAKE AWAY THE PAIN!......TAKE IT AWAY LAWD!...TAKE IT AWAAAAYYY!"

Annabelle stood there and prayed for several more minutes, afterward she returned back home to her mother. As she walked into the cabin, she could feel a calmness in the room, as if her mother was sleeping peacefully. She walked closer to where she was laying and looked down at her. As she began crying softly, she wondered to herself how she would ever be able to survive on that Plantation without her dear mother. Who would pray and give her the wisdom she needed to survive this hard life? Annabelle sat on the edge of the bed for a few seconds and stared down at the uneven floors. She layed beside her mother in that bed, wrapping her arms around her cold body tightly and cried herself to sleep.

The next day around noon, all Slaves from the Plantation gathered together at the burial site to say goodbye to Gladdia. They all stood around dressed in there black garments that were only worn for special memorials such as this one. Eliza and Annabelle stood beside one another holding hands while Noah and Jimmy stood behind Big Debra. They were comforting her as she prepared her mind mentally to sing Gladdia's favorite gospel hymn.

She looked around at the Slaves standing before her; then she looked out into the fields and saw Daniel. He was standing, dressed in his black garments with a bandage tied around his forehead from the night before. Big Debra stared at him for a moment, slowly shook her head from left to right, then opened her mouth widely and began to sing: "Precious Lord, take my hand."

Big Debra began singing with all of her heart and soul, there was hurt and passion in her voice and everyone felt it. Before she could sing the second verse of the hymn, she was interrupted by Shadrach; who suddenly decided to sing the verse himself. Everyone looked around at each other in shock as Shadrach song those lyrics as if his soul was being set free. Everyone was amazed.

Shadrach had been silent since the day he was captured as a runaway. Although Ola and Big Debra thought that he would never speak again, they smiled with tears in their eyes as his voice invited warmth in everyone's heart. Annabelle stopped crying and began smiling to herself. Deep in her heart she knew that her mothers' death bought healing and restoration to the Quarters. And as Shadrach and Big Debra song the last verse together, she was convinced that everything would be okay. Her mother was now her guardian angel.

After the memorial, all Slaves were ordered to there daily routines of working the fields. All house servants returned to the Plantation house. Annabelle and Eliza were ordered to gather up fruit and vegetables from the gardens, and they did so. As they were headed back to the Plantation house, walking through the fields, they began sharing a conversation with one another about the memorial,

"Be's a real nice service we has fo ya mama."

said Eliza,

"Real nice indeed. I looked down at her while she lay in the casket and it look like she was sound asleep."
Annabelle heard Eliza but did not show any emotion, she had a cold look on her face, as if her mind was full of thoughts,

"She be at peace nah."

she replied,

"Not in no mo pain, and no worries fo her."

"Well I saw the massa standing off into the fields!"

said Eliza,

 "Look like he take a nasty ole fall….or the mistress hit em upside the head wit a hickory stick."

Eliza began giggling, hoping that it lightened up Annabelle's mood, but it didn't, instead she became frustrated and replied angrily,

"Well if he did take a nasty ole fall…..it serve em right!....should thank the good lawd he not be dead!"

she said.

Eliza and Annabelle stopped walking for a moment and sat there basket of vegetables on the ground,

"Ya know it not be Christian to wish death on somebody."

 said Eliza,

"What's gotten into you gal!"

Annabelle stood with her hands on her hips, her facial expressions informed Eliza of her frustration, but she did not allow it to intimidate her, she stood and awaited her reply,

"Do you know what the massa did to me or my mama?"

said Annabelle,
"Ya know what he did before she died!.....huh?"

Eliza grabbed Annabelle by the hand,

"Well tell me what he did Anna!......did he hurt ya?.....make ya do bad thangs?"

 Annabelle didn't reply, she picked up her basket and headed   toward the Plantation house with Eliza following behind,

"No use in talkin bout it nah."

she said,

"Be's done and over wit."

Eliza was silent for a moment. She was concerned about Annabelle and what happened but did not want to upset her. Finally after a few more minutes of walking, she decided to ask her one last question,

"Well ya reckon the massa tries to hurt ya again Anna?"

Annabelle looked straight ahead with her lips squeezed tightly, as she often did when she became highly irritated. She walked and carried her basket, then replied to Eliza with a serious look on her face,

"Not less he plan on takin another nasty ole fall!"

she said,

"Best not come wit his trouble nothin!"

Eliza looked over at Annabelle from the corner of her left eye as they were walking through the field. Although she wasn't convinced, somehow she felt that Annabelle was hiding something from her; something that she did not want her to be aware of. But there was one thing that she was very certain of; although Daniel had the power to whip Annabelle at any given time, there was something mighty and something more powerful; a strong force in the heavens that wouldn't allow him to do so and they were both exultant in knowing that.

Later on that evening, Annabelle, Eliza, Ola and Jimmy were in the kitchen of the Plantation house sharing a conversation and working on their regular chores. If anyone would have enter the kitchen in that moment, they would have found Eliza standing at the stove stirring a pot of bisque and Ola at the sink washing dishes. Annabelle and Jimmy sat at the table eating apples and berries.

"Massa and Miss Patterson be getting ready for the big social in a few days."

said Jimmy,

"I hears em talking bout it the otha day, say folks from all the otha Plantations spose to be right here!"

As Jimmy spoke on the upcoming event, the others continue with their work duties, and pretended to not be concerned even though they were. They were listening carefully to every word.

"Don't know why Miss Patterson wonts to have all dem folk over here!"

replied Ola,

"Nothin worst than a bunch a white folk keepin up a buncha racket and drankin!"

Everyone nodded their head in agreement. As Jimmy was preparing himself to make one of his wise comments on the subject; Maryrose entered the room and suddenly he became nervous. Jimmy and Annabelle stood from the table at the same time and pretended to be working.

Maryrose looked at the both of them with more concentration on Jimmy. She reached for an apple and began eating it. She walked toward the kitchen window and looked out into the fields; this was usually an indication that she was about to either suggest something or make a wise comment. "Do believe yall spend too much time talking and not enough time workin!"

she said,

"LIZA!....when ya spose dinner be ready round here!....I'm hungry as a horse!"

Eliza looked up at Maryrose through the top corner of her eyelids while still stirring in the pot of bisque; making sure that it does not scorch,

"Reckon it wont be long ma'am."

she replied.

Maryrose ignored Eliza's response and walked toward the corner of the room. She looked around at everyone but stared mostly at Jimmy for a few seconds; it was as if she had something important going on in her mind.

"Anna!...needs ya to go tend to the living area, "Jimmy!....the storage shed needs tending to now!"

Maryrose said as she grabbed another apple from the table and walked out. Annabelle left to clean the living area as she was instructed. Jimmy left for the storage shed. Eliza and Ola remained in the kitchen and waited patiently for the opportunity to sneakily discuss what had just transpired.

Eliza stopped stirring the pot of bisque on the stove, ran to the doorway of the kitchen to make sure that there wasn't anyone listening or coming in. She ran over to Ola; who was still busy washing dishes and began to whisper,

"Know dere is somethin peculiar bout Miss Patterson…I knows it!"

Ola left the sink and walked over to the kitchen table to sit down, Eliza began washing the dishes that Ola left in the sink. As a house servant it was understood that work had to be completed at any cost; didn't matter who did it, as long as it was done. As Eliza began washing the dishes, she thought more about Maryrose, her strange behavior, and change of appearance.

"Sho do eat a lot round here."

she said,

"Like errytime I look up, she be hungry…eatin errythang in sight!...she always got us cookin extra food for her and she spreadin like butter…..dont reckon she…….."

As Eliza paused and thought for a moment, she looked over at Ola, hoping that she wouldn't say anything to confirm her thoughts. But she did.

"I don't reckon anything gal…I knows it!"

Ola replied,

"I been knowing for a while nah….has to be a fool not to see it. I prays the good lawd be wit Jimmy if the massa fine out!"

Eliza walked over to the table and sat down with Ola. She grabbed an apple and began eating it,

"Maybe errythang be okay."

she said,

"Maybe the massa be thinking the chile is his."

Ola looked across the table at Eliza as if she said something that was foolish and ridiculous,

"Oh hogwash!"

she replied,

"The minute that baby comes out black as led, massa gone have Jimmy strung up by a oak tree quick as you can slop a hog gal!….lawd I pray it not even be true, pray it not be true!"

As Eliza and Ola continued to work in the kitchen, along with Annabelle in the living area; Maryrose and Jimmy were secluded together in the storage shed. Jimmy sat there on a haystack looking down at the ground. He always felt guilty after having intercourse with Maryrose, only this time; he felt worst because she did not respond to him the way she usually does.

She positioned her dress on properly, pulled her hair behind her ears and stood near the entrance of the storage shed looking out into the yard. Jimmy walked over and stood beside her; putting his hands on her shoulders,

"Be's alright Miss Patterson?"

he asked; in a gentle warm voice.

"I be's alright."

Maryrose replied,

"Tired I guess and a lil confused."

Jimmy stood behind Maryrose; keeping his hand on her shoulders for comfort. Throughout the years Jimmy has grown emotionally attached to Maryrose. She was the first woman that he was sexually involved with. He was inlove with her. He looked at her with compassion in his heart and said,

"Whatever it is, you can talk to me bout it."

he said,

Maryrose turned away from the entrance and faced Jimmy. She had tears building in her eyes, this made him extremely nervous. In Williamsburg, tears usually indicated that there was something terribly wrong. Jimmy looked Maryrose in the eyes and waited anxiously for a response. She took a deep breath, grabbed him by his right hand and caressed it gently,

"If I tells ya something Jimmy, ya has to promise not to tell a soul, not even Big Debra can know bout this til the right moment."

Jimmy's heart began to beat faster than normal. The suspense was making him nervous by the minute.

"I swear to it!"

he said,

"Wont tell a soul to nobody."

Maryrose held her head down shamefully and began crying softly. She squeezed Jimmy's right hand tighter and began breathing harder. She was extremely upset at this point; yet she managed to utter these words to him,

"I be's wit-chile Jimmy."

Jimmy's heart filled with emotions. Did he hear her correctly? He could hardly believe what he heard come from Maryrose's mouth. He always imagined himself one day escaping to the North, marrying a beautiful woman and starting a family of his own. But this situation was entirely different. Not only was he sleeping with his Master's wife, there was also a strong possibility that she was carrying his child. This was a dilemma that could cost him his life. Jimmy looked at Maryrose surprised and confused,

"It....it be mine?"

he asked,

"God I pray it not be!"

said Maryrose,
   "But jus the same, best keep quiet bout this til I tell everyone, your life may depend upon it.....ya go on and leave now, git back to your chores."

   Jimmy stared at Maryrose for a moment, held his head down and slowly walked away from the storage shed; leaving her there alone.
   As she stood in the doorway of the shed, she began thinking about all the things that her mother taught her while she was alive. She thought about her life and how things could have been different if she would have never married Daniel. "Could things get any worst?" were the questions she asked herself over and over.
   The thought of carrying Jimmy's baby made her sick to the stomach, yet the thought of Daniel

finding out about their love affair caused her to feel terrified. She was determined to keep that secret to herself; but how long? There was only one thing left to do at that point; she made up in her mind that she would get rid of it. Although it was against what she believed in, she had to protect her reputation and Jimmy's life.

Later on that night, after everything had finally settled down; the Patterson's invited over Jackson and Elnora from the Richmond Plantation for a small dinner party. They were all gathered around the dinner table talking while Annabelle, Ola, and Eliza brought in dinner items from the kitchen.

"So how's our boy doin down there at Richmond?"

asked Daniel as he lit his pipe and took a sip of red wine.

"FINE!"

Jacskon replied,

"Jamison is doin quite well, he has learned the ways of Slave mastering quite rapidly; quicker than we anticipated."

Daniel and Maryrose looked across the table at one another and smile as Annabelle brought in another food item. She looked at Daniel unpleasantly from the corner of her eye. She never forgot what he did to her mother and father. The mere presence of him disgusted her, but she dare not say a mumbling word. Her only way of expressing her anger without words was through her eyes, which proved to be exceptional.

"Very well then Jackson!"

Daniel replied,

"Very well, nothing suits me more than to know my son is following my footsteps!"

"Oh indeed...INDEED!"

said Jackson,

"Jamison is a fine boy, will make ya both real proud."

The four of them sat at the dinner table and enjoyed their dinner. Jimmy stood at the entrance way of the room and awaited commands. Elnora, Jackson's wife looked over at Jimmy from the corners of her eye as if she knew something about him. She then looked over at Maryrose, who had guilt written all over her face. Elnora chose that opportunity to speak more about Jamison,

"Oh yes! We found great pleasure in having your son at Richmond Mary, it saddens us that soon he will have to leave......he's become much like a son of our own."

Maryrose looked over at Elnora and smiled without showing her teeth, she is aware that Elnora is extremely vigilant and nosy. Although she is extremely irritated by her, she continued to treat her with kindness,

"Well feel free to stop by and visit anytime Nora!"

Maryrose replied,

"You and Jackson are always welcomed!"

Maryrose began feeling sickly. She quickly stood from the table and wiped her mouth with a napkin, "If you all would excuse me, think I need a bit of fresh air."

She quickly walked out the dining area toward the kitchen. Jimmy followed her with his eyes as she left the room. Elnora noticed Jimmy looking at Maryrose and began to speak,

"Well everything sure does smell good doesn't Jackson?"

she said,

"Daniel, your servants do a remarkable job."

"Yes we have a balanced Plantation here."

said Daniel,

"We have to break a few down every now and then, but overall; dey do what's required of em. They are well disciplined."

Annabelle and the others began picking up dirty dishes and bowls from the table, Jackson took a sip of wine from his glass then looked at and Eliza and Ola,

"Ahhh yes! Dats the key to a flourishing Plantation."

he said,

"Well behaved Slaves!"

Jackson and Daniel both held their glasses in the air and tapped them against one another to signify a toast being made. As the three of them finished up their dinner and began feasting on the apple cobbler that was delivered to the table, they heard a loud sound coming from the kitchen. The sound was like someone had fallen from the roof, it startled everyone. They all stopped eating for a moment, and stood from the table. Suddenly they heard a voice crying out in the distance; it was Ola screaming to the top of her lungs,

"MASSA!...MASSA!....GIT HERE QUICK! SOMETHING
     BAD DONE HAPPEN!"

IX

Daniel and Jimmy left their guest at the dining room table and ran into the kitchen to investigate the commotion. They found Annabelle, Eliza and Ola standing over Maryrose as she was lying on the floor; she appeared to be extremely weak. Daniel leaned over Maryrose to take a closer look at her. He reached his hand toward her and with Jimmy's assistance; they lifted her from the floor. Annabelle, Eliza and Ola stood off to the side, they were more worried for Jimmy than Maryrose. There was something strange going on with her and the three of them knew exactly what it was. As Daniel and Jimmy positioned Maryrose in a chair, Daniel immediately began asking questions,

"Ola!...Anna!....what happened to her?

"Don't know massa"

replied Ola,

"She went for a glass of water and next thang ya know she black out and went fallin to the flow!"

Jimmy looked at Maryrose and began to worry for her. He knew that there was a possibility that she could be carrying his child. He did not want anything to happen to her or the baby. He was more concerned for her than his own life.

"Well yall come…help me git her upstairs to the bedroom."

replied Daniel,
"Liza!...go fetch Big Debra and tell her to hurry back here with her herbs."

Annabelle and Ola began to help Daniel with Maryrose while Jimmy went back into the dining area with Jackson and Elnora. Once he informed them of what happened, they gathered all of their things and left peacefully. Eliza ran as fast as she could through the Quarters; her and Big Debra were back at the Plantation house in less than thirty minutes.
When the two of them walked up the staircase, they found Daniel, Annabelle, and Ola standing outside of the bedroom door. Big Debra walked into the room with her medicine basket and closed the door behind her. When she walked in, she found Maryrose lying in bed on her side. Big Debra sat beside her and rubbed her forehead.

"So how long ya plan on goin on like dis without telling someone chile?"

said Big Debra.

"I'm afraid."

replied Maryrose,

"Maybe Daniel doesn't want another chile….maybe he feel a chile could get in the way of thangs…..was gonna ask ya to git rid of it for me."

"I can try mistress, but cant make no promises, somethin like dis has to be done at the very beginning, may be too late for ya."

replied Big Debra.

Big Debra stood from the bed and went inside of her medicine basket. She took out a jar with special ointment inside.

"Mistress, I needs ya to open your legs real wide for me, has to check ya to see how far along ya are."

she said.

Big Debra opened the jar and used her right hand to gently rub the ointment on Maryrose's vagina; she then took her left hand and slowly reached inside of her with two fingers. The procedure only lasted a few minutes, but slightly painful. Maryrose endured the pain. She was more concerned with getting rid of her problem that she created.

"So can you take care of it for me Big Debra?.....can ya git rid of it?"

cried Maryrose anxiously.

Big Debra walked toward the window of the bedroom; she did not want Maryrose to see the worry in her eyes. She knew that Maryrose was pregnant and that her son Jimmy could easily be the father. The thought of Daniel finding out made the two of them extremely nervous.

"Too late!...be about sixteen weeks"

replied Big Debra,

"If we try anything it could make ya real sick….may even kill ya!....ya have to let everything run its course ma'am….best ya go on and tell the massa….tell the massa there's a baby on the way."

Maryrose cried for a few minutes as Big Debra stood at the bedroom window silently. They both knew what they were facing and the consequences that could occur, however; there was nothing that could be done except praying that everything worked out for the good. Maryrose eased up on crying and asked Big Debra a question in a soft spoken voice, almost like a little girl asking for icecream.

"Ya think ya could go out and tell him for me?"

she asked.

Big Debra turned from the window and faced Maryrose,

"Spose I could go tell him for you."

replied Big Debra,

"I spec they all be standing outside in the hall waiting anyhow!"

Big Debra took a deep breath and wiped the tears from her eyes. She stared at Maryrose lying in bed and shook her head slowly. She walked toward the door, turned the knob slowly and walked out into the hallway where Annabelle, Eliza, Ola, Daniel and Jimmy were standing there waiting patiently. Big Debra held her head down, then lifted it slowly,

"She be wit-chile"

she said.

Jimmy, Annabelle, and Ola looked at one another with nervousness and fear in their eyes. Although there observations were true, the confirmation from Big Debra made things seem worst. Daniel was secretly excited. He silently walked inside of the bedroom and closed the door behind. Once he entered the room, he walked closer to Maryrose and sat on the edge of the bed,

"Gave us quite a scare there darling.....why on earth didn't ya tell me?"

Maryrose didn't say anything. She continued to lie on her side and stare at the wall. After a few moments of silence, she finally responded,

"I guess with all this running round gettn ready for the big social, I ran out of energy"

she replied,

"I....I been knowing bout the baby for sixteen weeks .....was worried bout how you would feel....didnt want ya mad at me."

Daniel began to feel more happy and excited inside, he looked at Maryrose with a big smile on his face,

"Well of course not!"

he said,

"I am the happiest man in Alabama right now...be bright around here with another youngin runnin round."

After hearing Daniel say those words, Maryrose felt a heavy burden lift from her shoulders; however she was still concerned about whom her baby's father was. She could not allow him to see the worry in her eyes. As she turned to face him, she looked him deep in his eyes, hoping that he would sense her vulnerability,

"So ya be's happy about the baby Daniel…ya really be's happy about it?"

she asked.

Daniel doesn't say anything else in that moment. He opens his arms and reaches for her to come closer to him. He embraces her with a warm hug and replies,

"Baby be jus what we need round here….be jus what we need."

As Maryrose layed her head in Daniels chest, a feeling of anxiety entered her mind. She was extremely happy that Daniel supported her pregnancy; however she knew deep in her heart that she did something cruel, something that she could never fix.

Maryrose deliberately slept with Daniel's most loyal servant Jimmy and now she was pregnant by him. Although Daniel spent years cheating on her by sleeping with other female Slaves, he would never forgive her if he found out about Jimmy. She made up in her mind to forget that it ever happened and to spend the next few months enjoying her pregnancy. It was her deepest wish that her secret affair would remain a thing of the past; and that this new addition would bring her and Daniel closer to one another.

Everyone with the exception of Big Debra and Jimmy returned to their household chores. The two of them snuck away quietly to the storage shed to have a private conference with each other, As they entered the shed, Big Debra immediately began lashing out at Jimmy.

"Look what you done went and did boy!"

cried Big Debra,

"You done went an made a mess of thangs round here!"

"It been goin on for a while nah mama, me and the mistress....kinda speck it would happen sooner or lata."

Jimmy replied.

Big Debra walked closer to Jimmy, he sat down on a haystack and looked toward the ground,

"THAT BE'S YO BABY MISS PATTERSON SPECTING!!!"

she asked.

Jimmy held his head up and answered with tears in his eyes,

"I don't know mama….not knows anything!....all I know is she always send fo me to meet her in here…say if I not lay wit her, bad thangs happen to Liza!....God I pray that baby not be mines mama!"

Big Debra listened to Jimmy's plea and walked to the other side of the shed. She held her head down and began crying for him. Jimmy heard her crying and rose from the haystack. He ran over to where she stood, took his finger and lifted her head up slowly,

"Don't cry for me mama…I find a way to make everything right…I find a way."

Big Debra took her hand and slightly gripped Jimmy around the cheek area of his face. She turned his head so that there eyes met with one another. she began to speak,

"Ya best hope dat baby not come out lookin like a niggra."
she said,

"Else massa kills you and dat baby!....I been on dis here Plantation a long time and I know!!....ya best stay far way from the mistress as ya can…we got dis social to git ready for and we don't need no mo trouble round here!!!"

After Big Debra spoke, she turned away from Jimmy and left him there alone. After she left, he stood there for a moment and thought about everything that occurred. Jimmy thought about what Daniel did to Maryrose, what Maryrose did to Daniel and what he done to the both of them. He could only ask himself, If this was God's way of punishing them all for their foolish behavior? At that moment, Jimmy was too ashamed to return back to the Plantation house that night. He decided that he would stay in the shed, and spend the remainder of the night talking to God until he fell asleep.

Later that night, Annabelle decided to take a walk through the fields. She brung along an old quilt incase she decided to rest a minute. As she walked throughout the land, she approached the fig tree where she and Jamison used to sit under when they were children. She stood there and stared at it for a few seconds, oh how she wish that she could turn back the hands of time. Things back then seemed so easy and less painful, she spread the quilt on the ground and sat down for a moment.

It had been four years since Annabelle had seen Jamison. The only memory she had of him was the day she watched a man drive him away. She often thought about the two of them together in the Plantation house, but she never took the time to enjoy all of the memories. Annabelle decided that this was her opportunity to enjoy them.

She layed down on the quilt and thought about all the times they shared together, from the time they were five years old, up until the time they were thirteen and shared there first piece of apple pie. She even thought about there first kiss. As she layed there thinking to herself a tear rolled down her cheek and she began to smile.

Although it was clear that she may not ever see Jamison again, one thing she was certain of was that they both loved each other very much, and nothing or no one could ever take her memories of him away. Annabelle fell asleep under the tree with nothing but happy thoughts to carry her throughout the night

Two weeks later, and the big day had finally arrived. Every Slave on the Plantation was up bright and early planning and getting things ready. They were all inside and outside of the house, moving furniture around, manicuring the lawn, trimming the grass and planting beautiful flowers. Maryrose and Daniel were running around giving orders and mentally preparing everyone for the big event that was scheduled to occur in just a few hours.

Maryrose had been planning this day all year long. It was a special occasion for her and Daniel. She wanted to be sure to make a good impression on her guests. She ordered new uniforms for all of her Slaves to wear so that everyone would look nice and professional. This also made them feel important and appreciated.

Everyone on the Plantation had a task, and they worked very hard to ensure that everything was in place and set up nicely. Within a matter of hours, the Williamsburg Plantation was turned into a beautiful yard festival. There were tables with

beautiful linen and center pieces, two people dressed as clowns and a live band playing dance music.
The sun was shining bright, which aided the yard in looking immaculate. Everything was going according to plan.

While all of the field Slaves were busy working outside, the house Slaves could be found in the kitchen, cooking, cleaning, and preparing food trays for the guests. And in between working, was a huge amount of talking,

"Lawd!..ya think afta all these years, Miss Patterson git right tide a feedin all dese people."

said Big Debra.

"Humph!...deys eat betta than we's do and we's the one who doin all the work round here!"

replied Hattie.

"Well yall best to git finished wit dem food trays!"

said Ola,

"Ya know the guest be showing up soon.....we gots to be up front at the door when dey walks in."
 Annabelle looked confused for a moment; this was her first time working the social without her mothers' guidance.

"What do I do?"

asked Annabelle,

"Laz time I not had to serve dem white folk….mama kept me in the kitchen to help her cook the food."

Eliza heard Annabelle's question and decided to do a demonstration and have a little fun in the process. She picked up a tray and began prancing around the room in a jokingly manner,

"It be easy Annabelle, ya jus pick up a tray like dis…and walk around the room like dis"

Once Eliza had everyone's attention in the room, she began to demonstrate even more; still prancing around the room,

"And ya smile real nice and big like this and ya ask em if dey wanna try something…… and when dey askya what it is; just tell em PIG FEET AND CHITTLINGS!"

Everyone in the kitchen, including Annabelle began laughing. In the midst of all their laughter, Maryrose stormed into the room with her stomach poking out. Everyone became quiet and continued working, not because they were afraid; but more in shock of how quickly Maryrose's stomach had grown. She grabbed some food from one of the food trays and pranced across the room as she normally does when there is an announcement to be made,

"Alright gals, guest are beginning to arrive, I needya to move quickly…don't have all day!...and who's spose to be serving at the door?"

"Me and Liza be serving ma'am."

 replied Annabelle.

"Well chop! chop!...lets git out there!..ya moves slow as molasses!"

said Maryrose as she stormed out of the kitchen door to greet her guest. Annabelle and Eliza looked at one another and just shook their heads slowly. They grabbed food trays and walked into the living area while the others stayed and prepared food items.

As Annabelle and Eliza walked into the living area with their food trays, they were amazed at what they saw. People were crowding the room by the bundles. Men were dressed in their fine suits, and the women had on beautiful custom made dresses; even their children were dressed to impress. The crowd in the room caused Annabelle to become slightly nervous, she had never been around so many Caucasian people in her life. It almost frightened her.

Eliza could tell that Annabelle was nervous, so every now and then she would look at her and smile. Although it was something so simple, it helped Annabelle to relax more and focus on her task without embarrassing herself. After a half hour of serving food trays, and listening to Maryrose thank everyone in the room for coming; she began to adjust herself. She actually enjoyed listening to the guest have conversation with one another and the sounds coming from the piano created a friendly atmosphere that she enjoyed.

As the crowd grew larger, Maryrose decided that it was a good time to make her grand announcement to everyone in the room. The piano stopped playing; Maryrose stood in the middle of the living area as the crowd circled in on her,

"MAY I HAVE EVERYONE'S ATTENTION PLEASE!!"

she yelled in a sweet tone,

everyone became quiet and then she continued,

"I jus wanna take time to thank all of you for coming out to my dinner and yard social. Hope everyone enjoy themselves…welcome…welcome….WELCOME!"

All guests in the room began to applaud Maryrose as she gave a small curtsey. Then the piano began playing and everyone continued socializing, laughing and drinking. The Slaves were walking at a steady pace, back and forth from the bar to the kitchen, replenishing drinks and food trays. The crowd of people was so large until Annabelle and Eliza hardly communicated with each other unless it was in passing. After a few hours of working, and serving all that food; Annabelle became hungry. She decided to take a small break in the kitchen while replenishing her food tray. As she walked into the kitchen, she almost bumped into Eliza as she was walking out,

"Gots to watch where ya be goin gal!"

 yelled Annabelle as she walked into the kitchen.

Ola and Hattie were in the kitchen, preparing food trays and laying them on the table. As Annabelle picked up a tray, she snuck a cheese cracker and tried to eat it. Ola slapped her hand and the cracker fell unto the floor,

"Miss Patterson catch u puttin yo hands on that food and she make ya throw the whole thang away….tray an all!"

said Ola.

Annabelle looked at Ola and giggled,

"Well what am I spose to eat when I get hungry….or is we spose to work all day and not eat!"

Ola pulled a tray of food from the refrigerator and sat it on the counter,

"We eat from dis tray!...I made it myself wit all the stuff I know Miss Patterson don't eat!"

 said Ola,

Hattie ran over to the kitchen door and peeped out to make sure that no one was coming; then she walked over near the food tray,

"Ya sho bout dat!"

said Hattie,
"Miss Patterson been walkin round here eatin errythang in sight, best to keep that tray hidden ALL DAY LONG!"

Annabelle, Ola and Hattie began eating from the food tray and laughing with one another. Suddenly they hear a loud scream coming from the living area,

"Now what in heaven is that noise, sound like Miss Patterson!"

said Annabelle.

Ola walked toward the kitchen door and peeped out,

"What is that white woman yellin about nah!"

 she said.

Annabelle grabbed another cracker and stuffed it in her mouth. She picked up her food tray and walked into the living area. The guests were crowded around the front door. Maryrose was screaming and kissing on what appeared to be a young Caucasian couple. The young man was very handsome and the young lady was beautiful with long red hair.

Ananbelle tried to walk closer, but the crowd made it almost impossible. She stood in one spot. These people must have been extremely important to Maryrose; Annabelle had never seen her look so happy; even the guests were applauding. As the crowd began to disperse, Annabelle was able to walk closer with her food tray, she was determined to find out who these people were, and why was everyone so excited to see them.

As Annabelle got closer to the crowd, she looked at the young couple standing near the front door and began feeling strange. She and the young gentleman stared into each others eyes for seconds. Those eyes looked so familiar to her. Where had she seen them before? Suddenly Annabelle's heart began to beat faster than normal. She became light headed and fainted. Annabelle fell unto the floor, dropping her food tray and causing a huge commotion. Everybody became disturbed and stood around Annabelle as she layed there unconscious with food everywhere.

The young gentleman at the front door became disturbed once he noticed Annabelle falling to the floor, he ran over and kneeled down beside her. He looked at her as she lied there with her eyes closed. He lifted her head with his hand and stared deeper into her face. He called out to her,

"Annabelle."

Although Annabelle was unconscious, she could hear the young gentleman calling her name. Who was this man and how did he know her? Was this one of the men who abused her? Was this someone who had been watching her? Unexpectedly; he called out to her again,

"Annabelle."

As Annabelle heard the young man's voice, something strange began to happen. Her heart filled with emotions and she began having small visions of when she was a little girl with Jamison. She dreamed of them running through the fields, sharing an apple pie and kissing under the fig tree. She also had a vision of what was happening in that moment when she collapsed. The young gentleman continued to call her name. The visions and the sound of his voice frightened her so badly until it caused her to regain consciousness. When Annabelle opened her eyes, she was short of breath, her heart was still beating at a fast pace and she wanted to speak but had difficulty. She looked up and noticed people standing around looking down at her. She heard whispering voices, Maryrose yelling in the background, but more importantly she saw a young handsome man holding her in his arms, and he was calling her name.

As tears filled her eyes, she took a second to thank God for answering her prayer. Throughout every bad thing that she experienced on the Plantation, he cared enough to give her a personal gift and allow the true love of her life to return home. There he was, right before her very eyes, and he was calling her name. She recognized that it was unfeigned. Annabelle looked that young gentleman in the eyes, took a deep breath, and then she answered him calmly,

"Jamison!"

It was that moment when the two of them realized that their love was unconditional. No matter the situations or circumstances that they faced in their lives, their faith conquered them all. The two of them were together again, Finally.

www.ingramcontent.com/pod-product-compliance
Lightning Source LLC
Chambersburg PA
CBHW031247170626
46807CB00001B/21